He want

The thought came like a warm breeze across her body. As Chris neared the shore, he scooped her up in his arms, walking toward the boathouse. "You ever made love in a hammock before?"

Lucy looked up thoughtfully, hoping he couldn't tell her heart was beating so fast. "Nope, can't say that I have."

"Well, then, let me initiate you." He deposited her in the hammock, not even waiting for it to stop swinging before dropping down on top of her.

The sun shone in the window next to them, lighting his green eyes to match the sparkling water outside. She reached up and placed her palms on either side of his face as he worked her wet skirt down.

He nibbled across her skin while his fingers took her right to the edge of ecstasy. She could feel the soft tip of him sliding up and down her thigh, and she was sure she'd never wanted a man the way she wanted Chris.

A sound escaped her mouth as she arched and drowned in waves of pleasure. He made a similar sound when she reached for him, gliding her fingers up and down the length of him in a slow rhythm that coincided with the swinging of the hammock....

Dear Readers,

Readers often wonder where authors get their ideas. *The Best of Me* was inspired by a news story on the show *Inside Edition*. Ric O'Barry, the man who trained the original *Flipper* dolphins, now spends his life fighting for the rights of captive dolphins. In the news story he had gained custody of a dolphin in Brazil and was repatriating him to the wild. I, like many people, am mystified by the dolphin, so a man who sacrifices his own personal happiness and well-being to save them is a hero in my book. Through a series of quirky events, I was able to meet Ric O'Barry. Not only was he fascinating, but his book, *Behind the Dolphin Smile* was an important resource. I thank him for his invaluable help, and for being a hero in the truest sense of the word.

I must also extend my gratitude to Bill, who spent time with me at Key West Aquarium showing me how an aquarium works, even the back rooms no one usually sees.

Now, for my fictional hero Chris Maddox, I needed a match, a woman who was strong, yet tender enough to touch my jaded hero's heart. Of course, she's also his total opposite. But these two people bring out the best in each other and make them question the things they hold dear.

Tina Wainscott

P.S. Please visit my Web site! www.tinawainscott.com

THE BEST OF ME
Tina Wainscott

HARLEQUIN®

TORONTO • NEW YORK • LONDON
AMSTERDAM • PARIS • SYDNEY • HAMBURG
STOCKHOLM • ATHENS • TOKYO • MILAN • MADRID
PRAGUE • WARSAW • BUDAPEST • AUCKLAND

My deepest gratitude to Ric O'Barry, founder of the
Dolphin Project. This book would not have existed
without him. And for all the heroes who work to
free captive dolphins. Those heroes include the ones
who work in the background, who support the
Dolphin Project and similar organizations,
and everyone who picks up a pen
to write to someone who
can make a difference.

ISBN 0-373-25994-8

THE BEST OF ME

1

LUCY DONOVAN pulled her luggage beneath the arched, faded sign that read, Sonny's Marine Park—See Randy the Dolphin! She took a deep breath and stared at the first word because Sonny wouldn't be there. Her father had died, leaving the daughter he'd hardly spoken with in twelve years his park in Nassau, Bahamas. She felt silly at the sting of tears behind her eyes, at the deep sense of loss. She'd hardly known him.

According to her mother, Sonny was a lazy, good-for-nothing bum. To Lucy, he was a free spirit, an explorer, maybe even a pirate. Though her life reflected her mother's values, somewhere in Lucy's soul flowed the blood of the great adventurer she imagined him to be.

She swiped at her eyes and forged on. The ticket booth doubled as a gift shop with displays of key chains and shells. A young man with brown hair nodded as she approached.

"Hi, I'm Lucy Donovan, Sonny's daughter. I'm supposed to see a Bailey."

His face broke into a smile that combined relief and welcome. "Boy, are we glad to see you, Lucy, and welcome to Sonny's. I'm Bill. Bailey's in the office over there."

"Thanks, Bill."

She paused just inside the gate, finding it hard to believe she owned this park right on the ocean. To her left, several in-ground pools sparkled in the sunshine, one with a group of people clustered around it. A sign announced a square tank of water as the Touching Tank. People picked up conch shells and crabs and examined the creatures with wonder. Everyone made her feel overdressed, even though she'd taken off her linen jacket the moment she'd stepped off the plane and succumbed to the muggy heat.

She headed to a small building snugged next to a larger one with a sign over its gaping entrance that read Aquariums. Inside the office, a thin black man stood by a battered desk, rubbing his temples and clutching the phone. The desk and shelves were cluttered with papers and seashells.

The man picked up a letter. "But dere has to be some mistake, mon. Yah, I see the man's signature, but...so I cannot even shoot him? Okay, okay. No, I won't shoot him, I promise." The lyrical way he spoke made her smile despite his annoyance. He dropped the phone into the cradle.

She stepped forward, her hand extended. "You must be Bailey. I'm Lucy Donovan, Sonny's—"

"A yu, Miss Lucy! Yah, I see Sonny in you, same brown eyes and hair, same length, too." She touched her shoulder-length hair, but he rambled on. "Am I glad to see you, yes I am. We have a problem, a big problem. The man out dere is tiefing da big fish. A wicked man, dat one. He come dis morning and say he taking our fish. Nobody will come to da park if dere's no big fish, and without people you got no money, no money means no park, and no park means no job, no job means no food. I got five childrens to feed, an' t'ree goats." He took a deep breath. "Miss Lucy, you got to kick the wicked man outta here."

Cleaning out her father's place and deciding what to do about the park she now owned was part of her agenda. So was finding out what her father was really like at the risk of her fanciful dreams. Kicking out some wicked man was not on the list of things she wanted to tackle.

"You said a man was tiefing?"

"Tiefing. Stealing. He be taking our main fish, Randy. Come, I show you."

"Wait a minute," she said, but he kept walking. "How can someone steal a fish?"

She followed him toward the cluster of people. All she knew about fish was to make sure it was fresh and thoroughly cooked. This knowledge probably wasn't going to help much. But she did know subordinate workers.

She slipped on her jacket, effecting her boss persona, and asked Bailey, "Does anyone else work here?"

"No, jus' me, Bill, and Big Sonny, him being in da past tense of course."

The crowd mumbled and grumbled. "Hey, we paid to see a perr-formin' dolphin," a large man drawled. "That guy says we can't go near him. What kind of deal is this, anyway?"

"Yeah, I want my money back," another chimed in.

"Me, too! I heard about these island rip-off artists."

"Nooo, no rip artists here, mon." Bailey turned to give her a woeful look, then raised his palms and turned back to the crowd. "We're working on da problem, mon. Go play wit' da conchs and crabs in da Touching Tank, and we get da big show ready. Go, go," he said, wiggling his fingers.

They moved away, but didn't leave. Obviously they thought a better show was about to be performed. Lucy's throat went dry, but anger prickled through her at the thought of some man stealing the main attraction. What nerve. She pushed back her sleeves and stepped up to the knee-high fence that surrounded all the pools.

The man standing in chest-deep water on a platform paid absolutely no attention to anything but the large form circling in the pool with him. He was probably in his early thirties, with blond hair burnished gold by the sun. His curls grazed the tops of strong, tan shoulders. Quite possibly he had one of the nicest chins she'd ever seen, strong and perfectly shaped. Something warm tickled through her. He could be an attraction himself: See Gorgeous Guy in Pool!

Bailey nudged her, and she blinked in disbelief. Good grief, she was supposed to kick the man out, not ogle him!

"Excuse me," she said, leaning over the fence. "Man in the pool."

The man pulled a fish out of a bucket. The big fish moved closer and popped its head out of the water. Oh, it was a dolphin like Flipper! Ridges of tiny teeth lined its open mouth, and for a moment she worried about the man's long fingers. The big fish caught its supper in midair, landing with a graceful splash. The crowd clapped sporadically, but the man didn't even glance up.

"Excuse me," she said, louder this time. "Please get out of the pool so we can discuss this."

He glanced up at her then, insolence in vivid eyes the color of the sparkling ocean beyond him. She felt her stomach twist. Before she could even admonish herself for getting caught up in his eyes, he'd turned back to the dolphin.

The pattern in the concrete made her heels a little shaky, but she stepped over the gate and the sign he'd obviously put up that said Keep Out, and walked to the edge. No one ignored Lucy Donovan. Running her own advertising company had given her an edge of authority, and if she could get past those eyes, she'd have him bowing in acquiescence in no time. The thought of him bowing in front of her also did strange things to her stomach.

She planted her hands on her hips, and in her best bosslike tone, said, "Out of the pool now, mister."

"Lady, if you're not careful, you're going to end up in the pool. Some of the tiles around the edge are loose."

"You think you can scare me away with a few loose tiles?" She glanced back at the crowd that probably thought this was some kind of skit. "Who are you and what right do you have to be in this pool? This is private property." Her private property.

The dolphin popped out of the water and caught the fish again. The crowd clapped. Anger surged. Forget his eyes! This guy *is* wicked, she thought, walking around to the side behind the dolphin.

"I want an answer or I'm calling the authorities."

"I already explained everything to that guy," the man said, waving vaguely toward Bailey but not looking at anyone but the big fish.

She crossed her arms in front of her chest. "Since I'm the owner, why don't you explain it to me?"

The strength from her last statement trickled away when he turned those eyes on her, and she saw disgust. "You're the owner?"

Her shoulders stiffened. "Yes. And I want to know why you're molesting my fish."

Well, now she had his attention. He swam toward her, the sun glistening off his wet shoulders. She sensed a fight brewing and geared her body toward it. In one slick movement he shoved himself out of the pool and stood to face her. Or look down at her, as it were. Water ran in rivulets down a chest sprinkled with fine, golden hair. He wore one of those little swimming trunk things that outlined everything, and she wasn't going to look anymore. On a black cord around his neck he wore a shark's tooth. She looked up to meet his eyes, refusing to be intimidated by him, his height, or his eyes. Or what the deep blue trunks revealed. A warm breeze washed over her, making her aware of the fine sheen of perspiration on her face.

He crowded closer into her zone. "First of all, that is not a *fish*. He's a mammal like you and me, only not as selfish and greedy and inhumane. That dolphin has been living in a chlorinated pool that has bleached his skin white and has made his eyes nearly close. Dolphins are made to swim out there." He gestured toward the open ocean. "Not in that little swimming pool. His snout's beat up from bumping against the sides. This very social creature has lived alone for six years. His only company is some guy who makes him do tricks for a bunch of people who think it's neat to see a dolphin jump and twirl for his meals, which have, up until today, consisted of frozen mullet. To you and me, that's like eating dog food. Frozen dog food."

She didn't think it was possible, but he moved even closer. "You have stripped from that dolphin everything that makes him a dolphin. His pod and all the hierarchy and social activities that go with it, the thrill of the chase, the feel of the open, endless ocean, the fun of life, and if you want to get right down to it, you've robbed his soul. He was going to die in that pool, and you would have been responsible. My name is Chris Maddox. I'm the founder of the Free Dolphin Society, and I've been given authority by the Bahamian government to repatriate this dolphin to the wild."

He touched his finger to her collarbone, sending little shock waves through her chest. "I'm not going anywhere without this dolphin. Got it?"

Anger turned to guilt as his words spiked through her. She shifted away from him—and something moved under her heel. The tile tilted, and she lost her balance. Arms flailing, she fell toward the sparkling water with that huge form moving beneath it. Dignity be damned, she thought, as a scream tore from her throat. Her fingers slid across Chris's slick skin as she tried to grab for anything. She felt his hands on her arms, but it was too late. Momentum was doing its thing, and they both tumbled into the pool.

She came to the surface with a loud gasp, shoving herself toward the shallow platform. Chris came up a second later, flicking his head back and sending a spray of water behind him. And the big fish...the dolphin swam toward her.

She felt her eyes bulge out in panic. "Get it away from me!"

When she turned to Chris for help, her fear bubbled to anger. He was laughing! Then the sound of more laughter filled the air. She turned toward the clapping crowd. The only person not laughing was Bailey. He looked shell-shocked. She pressed her palm to her forehead, and then realized she was still in the pool with the big fish. Its head was now out of the water, and even it seemed to be grinning at her.

"This is not funny," she said to no one in particular, pushing wet strands of hair from her face. She hated the tremble that crept through her voice. "Just keep that fish away from me."

"He's not a fish, he's a dolphin," Chris corrected again,

though he still had the same kind of grin on his face the dolphin had.

"Fine, please keep the dolphin away while I get out of here."

Her linen pants felt leaden as she turned to the side of the pool. Earlier he had pressed down on the edge and lifted himself right out of the water. But he wasn't wearing wet pants or heels, and she didn't have the muscles he did.

"Need some help?"

"No, I've got it."

She kicked off her expensive, and ruined, pumps and threw them onto the concrete deck. Then she pushed up on the edge. If only she could manage a shred of dignity...that was not to be the case, she realized as she shoved and grunted and not even Bailey moved from the spot he seemed riveted in.

"Let me help you," Chris said from behind her.

"I can manage. It's just that my pants are heav—"

Before she could even finish the sentence, he placed his hands on her behind and pushed her right out of the water. She was so surprised, she almost forgot to do her part, which was grab for the ground and gain her balance. Even then, she could still feel the imprint of his hands on her bottom.

"I'm not sure whether to thank you for being gallant or remark on where you put your hands," she said, feeling irritated and flustered at once.

A wicked gleam sparked in his eyes as he slipped easily from the pool. "I enjoyed it, too."

She could only roll her eyes at his attempt to goad her on. When she looked at the small crowd watching with interest, she realized she'd become the sideshow at her own park.

"Bailey, please get these people out of here," she said, trying not to sound impatient and out of sorts.

He jerked, as if from a trance. "Yes, Miss Lucy, right away." Before he turned toward the crowd, he said, "Don't let him take da fish. Remember my six childrens at home starving."

"You said five before."

His black face screwed up. "Did I? Well, six counting da goat."

"You said you had three goats."

He paused for a minute, then smiled. "Two are only visitin'."

She shook her head and waved him away. When she turned back to Chris, he was watching her with a curious expression. At least he wasn't crowding her zone. She knew about business power plays and how body zones worked, and she didn't much like when they were used on her.

"Can we go into the office and talk about this like two businesspeople?" she asked, trying to ignore the rivers of water running down her legs and pooling at her stocking feet.

He glanced down at his nearly naked self. "In case you hadn't noticed, *Miz* Lucy—" that last part in Bailey's accent "—I'm not a business person, and this isn't negotiable. I gave your employee the letter that states the dolphin is mine. That should clear the matter up." Then he slid back into the pool in one liquid movement and waded to the bucket of fish. She followed him and crouched by the side, careful of the edge this time.

"What you said about this dolphin, about the chlorinated pool, and the snout...."

"What you're doing to this dolphin is cruel and inhumane. Liberty—or Randy as you call him—wasn't put on this earth to entertain us. Dolphins are probably smarter than we are. How would you like to live in something like this day in and out, eating trash fish, and having to suffer the indignity of performing to get even that? To look at white walls instead of the endless variety the ocean and the reefs offer?"

Liberty poked his head out of the water as if to second Chris's words, or probably to get the shiny fish he held. Her heart twisted when she saw the bruises on Liberty's snout. Then she realized that Chris thought she was the one who had been running this park all along.

"I haven't done anything to this dolphin."

"You said you were the owner."

"I just inherited it from my father, Sonny Boland. I didn't even know he owned this park, or where he even was for most of my life." Why was she telling him all this? *Stick to the facts, Lucy.* "Anyway, I arrived today, and Bailey told me about a man stealing a big fish." He rolled his eyes, and she added, "I know, I know, it's a dolphin."

He reached out to touch Liberty, but the dolphin shied away. Another fish lured him close again, but Chris didn't try to touch him this time. He was again immersed in his world, and she had faded into oblivion. If she had any dignity whatsoever, she would walk away. Just get up and hold her soggy shoulders high. Unfortunately, her curiosity overwhelmed any shred of dignity she'd managed to maintain.

"Why do you call him Liberty?" She glanced up at the banner. "His name is Randy."

"Calling dolphins by human names encourages people to humanize them, so I renamed him Liberty."

"What are you going to do with him?" she asked after a few awkward minutes of silence. She wanted to change into dry clothes, but she couldn't leave without his acknowledging that she wasn't an evil person who abused dolphins. Though she didn't explore why that was so important.

"I have to untrain him, teach him how to catch live fish and to live in the wild again. He's come to depend on humans and their language now. He has to learn to be a dolphin again, to use his sonar."

He hadn't glanced up at her even once as he'd spoken. She wanted to see something other than disdain in his eyes. She ran her hands down her pant legs, squishing water out of them.

"What do you mean, his sonar?"

His fingers made circles on the water's surface. "Dolphins use echolocation sonar to map out their surroundings the same way we use our eyes. They send out signals that bounce back to their lower jaw, telling them where they are and where their prey is. Here in this shallow pool, the signals bounce crazily back to him, so he stopped using them."

Sonar? It sounded so high-tech, so...advanced. She watched Liberty circle, trying to imagine what he saw down there. White walls. Chris's legs. "Is there anything I can do to help?"

The sun glistened off his wet curls as he shook his head. "Just leave me and Liberty alone, and we'll be fine."

He hadn't even thanked her for offering. Still hadn't looked at her. He reached for Liberty, and again the dolphin shied away. As she watched Chris, she wondered if her father wasn't like him, other than the dolphin-saving thing.

"Is this what you do for a living? You said something about a free dolphin society."

"I *am* the Free Dolphin Society. I travel around to different abusement parks and work on freeing the dolphins trapped there."

"Abusement parks? Is that what this is?"

"For this dolphin, yes. I don't know how the other creatures are treated."

She looked around, but couldn't tell from where she was crouched. The park looked clean, if old. "Do you think my father was being cruel or just thoughtless?" She was surprised to find him looking at her when she turned back to him. More surprised at the effect that gaze had on her.

"I only met the man once, when I first came to investigate claims of neglect. It was probably a little of both. Liberty here eats about fifteen pounds of fish a day, so Sonny bought the cheap stuff. He didn't want to mess with filtering in fresh seawater or even making phony salt water, so he put chlorine and copper sulfide in the pool. Your father was upping the profit margin, and Liberty was paying the price. Now I'm pumping in seawater, and hopefully he'll be able to open his eyes all the way soon."

"Will he bite? I mean, was I in any danger when I fell in?"

A smirk tugged at the edges of his mouth, and she bet he had a great smile, if he ever did smile. Of course he was probably laughing at her expense, remembering how she must have looked, all arms and legs and terror.

"The only thing in danger was your dignity. Dolphins are pretty docile in captivity." He tossed Liberty the last of the fish in the bucket and rubbed his hands together under the water. He lifted an eyebrow. "Wouldn't your spirit be broken if you were held captive?"

She shivered at the thought, watching Liberty as he

waited patiently for more fish, his head bobbing. "Probably," she answered at last, meeting Chris's gaze across the sparkling water. "Dolphins are your life, aren't they?"

"Yep." Chris lifted himself from the pool and grabbed a towel. "How long are you here for, anyway?"

"A week. It's all I can get away with."

He nodded, rubbing the towel through his curls. Then she realized he only wanted to know how long he had to put up with her. When he stopped near her, he looked down at the clothing plastered to her body. She wasn't sure if she imagined the gleam of appreciation, but he offered her his towel before she could consider it further.

She lifted the soggy towel with her fingertips. "Your chivalry touches me, to be sure, but I think you've just about used up all the saturation." She handed it back.

He shrugged in a suit-yourself way, removed a pair of shorts and a cotton shirt from his duffel bag, and shoved the towel inside. "I'm just a gallant kind of guy." He stepped into the shorts and slid his feet into leather sandals. Golden hair sprinkled his long, lean legs. The muscles in his arms moved intriguingly as he shrugged into the button-down shirt, though she was trying hard not to look. She met his gaze and found that smile she'd been wondering about. Yep, heart tickling all the way down to her toes. "Take it easy."

Like a fool, she watched him go, watched what might possibly be the cutest derriere in the world walk away. He walked through the gate and mounted a moped. Never once did he look back. Not even a furtive side glance while her gaze was glued to him.

Well, what was she in a snit about? Because he'd been as clear as the sky that he didn't want her around? Not a man of subtleties and courtesy, that one. She could take a hint. Lucy Donovan did not go where she wasn't wanted. She hadn't hung around in her marriage once it was old and stale and she wasn't about to hang around Chris Maddox, either.

Lucy had a feeling it went beyond that, though. Chris Maddox simply didn't want people around. And now she had to wonder why.

2

CHRIS WEATHERED the rocks and dips in the narrow road as he sped toward The Caribe Plantation. The other drivers were the biggest hazard. His clothes flapped in the wind, the tips of his shirt snapping against his skin. The Caribe was just down the road from the park, a mere fifteen life-threatening minutes away. The plantation wasn't in the touristy area of the island, something Chris was grateful for.

The plantation's driveway was crushed shell, pristine white for those times when the Eastor family vacationed at their Colonial mansion on the ocean. Luckily they weren't there, and even luckier, they had offered their grounds and lagoon to his cause. He wasn't impressed by the flowering gardens and trees; what mattered was the private slice of azure water where Liberty would learn to be a dolphin again. He barely glanced at the mansion as he headed to the hut perched over the water that doubled as a boat dock—and constituted his accommodations.

Through the traffic and roar of wind in his ears, it was Lucy Donovan's face he had seen and tried to exorcise. Lucy with her brown hair plastered to her cheeks and framing her dramatic features. He caught himself smiling at the terror in her face when she'd fallen into the pool. He shook his head as he parked the bike and made his way over the boardwalk that led out to the boathouse.

Lucy with her brown eyes that shadowed when he'd accused her of her father's neglect. He knew she had nothing to do with Liberty's plight, because he'd investigated the park and found no Lucy anywhere. He'd only wanted to rattle her—and get rid of her.

The last thing he needed was a woman hanging around. Women didn't take being ignored for long, especially a woman like Lucy Donovan. He could tell she was a lady who required care and attention. In her fancy suit and nice jewelry, she reeked of class. He hadn't seen a ring on her finger, and he wasn't going to bother exploring why he'd even looked. She wasn't going to go for a quick fling with the likes of him. Besides, she wasn't the type of woman he'd think about having a quick fling with.

But he was.

His body stirred as he walked around to the back of the boathouse and stripped out of his shorts and swimsuit. The freshwater shower faced the open ocean, which was free of anything but clouds piling up in the distance like whipped cream on a sundae. He rubbed the shampoo through his hair and focused his thoughts on the weeks ahead.

And again his thoughts settled back on Lucy. What was the point? He'd snubbed her but good, and tomorrow she'd return the favor. That's how women were. Besides, she was no great beauty. Pretty, definitely, with a heart-shaped face and thick eyebrows. Full breasts molded by the wet shirt, the peaks of her nipples evident even through her lacy bra. A mouth that could have a man fantasizing in no time. And that derriere of hers, soft and shapely and fitting perfectly in his hands. He'd been going for the economy of the move; the rest was a bonus.

Forget about that derriere and the woman it belongs to. He directed that to his male member that obviously thought he was on vacation—and forgot that he was thirty-six. He thought of those few hello-goodbye affairs with women who lived by the ebb and flow of the islands. Lucy was a city girl. City and island didn't jibe.

A seagull shrieked as it hovered nearby. Creatures of nature were his only friends. He found them easier to understand than people. Easier to live with. His passions didn't leave room for a woman in his life. He knew he'd never find a woman who would share his dedication to saving dolphins, who would sacrifice a secure, stable life for the cause. A woman who would be okay with coming second to it.

It was easier to be alone.

He had grown up in a world that lacked compassion. His mother died when he was too young to remember, leaving his father bitter and cold. He'd lived only for his fishing charter business. He catered to his guests and criticized them later. All he cared about was having enough money to continue living on the boat and buying the beer he subsisted on...the beer that would later claim his liver, and his life. Chris had been a means to that end, a hardworking employee who found his only joy in the sea life around him.

After his shower, he stretched out on his lounge chair. He'd flown in that morning, found the Caribe, then went to the park to work on phase one: gaining Liberty's trust. He should be exhausted, and lying down doing nothing sounded wonderful.

Exactly two minutes later, he was up again.

Restlessness ran through him. He walked to the beach, measured out where Liberty's pen would go, and stretched out nets and floaters along the beach like some sea monster washed up on shore. When it was too dark to work, he took a ten-minute ride farther south down the winding road that followed the coastline to Barney's Happy Place for a Red Stripe beer. Maybe that would purge Lucy and her incredible derriere from his mind.

LUCY HAD finally wrenched herself away from watching Liberty, changed into dry clothes, and found Bailey hosing down the cement walkways.

"You didn't chase the wicked man away?" he asked.

"No, and honestly, I don't want to."

He shook his head. "I see the way you look at him. What a crosses! Our only hope, and she fall for the wicked man!"

"What are you talking about?" She'd only looked at his eyes maybe once or twice. Only been slightly bewitched by them.

He shook his head. "Everyt'ing gonna go down the drain now dat your pupa is gone." He nodded toward the drain the water swirled down.

Guilt nagged at her when she thought of his six—no five kids. "What would my father—pupa have done?"

"He would have punched the wicked man out who tief the big fish."

"He's not a fish," she said.

"Cho, now you even sound like the tief!"

She rolled her eyes, glad not to have to put up with such insubordination back home. "My father would have been arrested for punching him out. Besides, Chris Maddox says he has authority. Is that true?"

"He must have tickled dere noses with a bit of cash."

Somehow she doubted that. "Well, why don't you show me the books? Let's see if my father had a head for business."

The books did not look healthy, she soon found out.

No wonder Sonny only had two employees. When she propped her chin on her hand, she caught sight of a small photograph on a shelf. She walked over and picked up the dusty frame, surprised to see her own childish face smiling at her. Something tightened inside her. Sonny hadn't forgotten her after all.

"Miss Lucy, I be ready to leave now. You want me to take you where Sonny live?"

"Yes, please."

Bailey drove her south on a winding road in need of some repairs—and police supervision. The drivers were crazy, regularly crossing the centerline or stopping for no apparent reason.

"The rich people buy the fancy places and only live in them a few weeks a year," Bailey said, pointing to some elaborate entrances on the ocean side of the road. "Everybody else live over dere." The housing to her left was lower- to middle-class. People sat out on rickety front porches watching the traffic while goats grazed on weedy front yards. She shifted her gaze to the right side and caught sight of an entrance proclaiming The Caribe Plantation in discreet lettering.

Bailey turned shortly after that and pulled up to a pink three-story building with thick white balconies. Sonny's apartment was a one-bedroom efficiency, a hot, stuffy one at that. She turned on an air conditioner unit installed in the window. She was beginning to regret her decision to stay there while she packed up his belongings, practical though it was.

If she'd hoped to find traces of her father here, she was out of luck. Against one wall were shelves of broken tanks and pump parts he'd obviously intended to fix. The furnishings were sparse, old, but clean. The junk food that had been behind his heart attack filled the shelves.

She found a stack of wrinkled, water-stained Caribbean maps covered in notations. She ran a finger over his small, neat script. He'd found pleasure in nature, apparently, noting various reefs and abundant water life.

It was after eight-thirty when she dropped onto the old green sofa. Her foot pushed in a drawer in the coffee table, and she pulled it open. Yellowed newspaper clippings were piled up inside. She sifted through them, her throat tightening. They were all of her, graduating college, getting married, opening the advertising firm.

Sonny had kept up with her life from a distance. She felt like crying and smiling at the same time. If he'd known about her wedding, why hadn't he written? At least he hadn't known about her divorce.

Lucy peeked out of the listless curtains and watched people come and go at the nearby store. She had to get out for a while, breathe some of that fresh, salty air, and think things through. Bailey had said the neighborhood was safe, so Lucy pocketed some cash and walked into the starry night air. The muggy, starry night, she amended, as moisture wrapped around her. She'd been so busy fighting with Chris, and then with the numbers, she hadn't begun to appreciate the island.

She walked along the ocean side of the road and headed south to a place Bailey had recommend for "da best ribs on the island." Her stomach gurgled at the aroma of spices and hickory smoke emanating from Barney's Happy Place. She paused, trying to judge the clientele by the exterior. Barney's was right off the road, perched several yards from the ocean, or what she guessed was the ocean beyond the sandy shore that turned to inky darkness. The place looked like a large shack, with its faded wood and half walls. Reggae music tainted the night air with a festivity punctuated by the red, yellow and green Christmas lights strung outside. Palm trees rustled in the evening breeze, cast in the glow of those lights. Her parents and ex-husband would be horrified to know she was going into a place like this. She smiled and walked up the ramp.

She almost walked back out again when she saw all the people. Many looked like locals, dressed in colorful garb, their heads adorned with dreadlocks and cornrow braids. Barney's was not a tourist hangout, to be sure, except for one couple that sat at a corner table with frou-frou drinks and burned noses. Music rivaled the laughter and conversation that flowed out the back, which was entirely open to the beach beyond.

A long bar stretched out to the right where a bartender was telling a joke, using his hands and face for expression. The people sitting on the stools laughed in unison. She took a deep breath. *Be adventurous. You can tell everyone you went into a real island joint.*

Yeah, like they'd believe her.

She made her way to the bar. At least she had brought her one pair of shorts and a tailored shirt with short sleeves. She slid onto the padded stool.

The bartender flopped a red napkin in front of her. "And what have you, miss?"

What was it with the "misses" around this place? First Bailey, then Chris's mimicked version and now the bartender. She realized that she'd been ensconced in her own little world where she was in control. No one there would dare call her Miss Lucy, nor would they ignore her. "I'll have a frou-frou drink like that couple is having." She watched him splash several liquors into a glass with the grace of someone who loved his job.

"Well, well, if it isn't Miz Lucy herself hanging out with the locals."

Her heart lurched at the sound of Chris's voice, but she attributed it to surprise and turned to the man at her left. She let her gaze drop from his curly hair to the tank top and jean shorts he wore. To cover what she hoped wasn't appreciation in her eyes, she said, "So that's what you look like with clothes on."

The bartender chose that moment to bring her drink. "Ah, so you know the lady already," he said to Chris with a smile and a wink.

Her face went up in flames. "No, I didn't mean it like that. He was in the pool...."

The bartender waved his hand. "No problem, lady. The island bring out the animal in lots of people."

"But—" The man had already walked away, and she turned to Chris who was chuckling. She narrowed her eyes. "Don't move too fast to defend my honor, now. I wouldn't want you to hurt yourself."

He shrugged. "Hey, I'm way out of practice coming to a lady's defense."

She rolled her eyes. "To be sure."

"So what if he thinks we've had a round or two of wild, steamy sex? He's a bartender in a foreign country." He gestured toward the lot of people behind him. "Probably sees illicit affairs all the time."

Wild, steamy sex...just the thought of it sent blood rushing through her veins. She was not, absolutely *not*, picturing him on the other side of that steamy sex scenario. "But we are *not* having a steamy affair, I have *not* seen you naked, and I don't want him thinking I have."

He leaned one arm against the bar, facing her. Those green eyes had a lazy glaze to them, probably from those Red Stripe beers he was drinking. "Would you like to?"

"What?"

"See me naked?"

A tickle raced through her stomach even as she made a face and turned to her monstrous pink drink with the umbrella in it.

"Given that tiny bathing suit you wear, I don't have to see you naked." *Oh, that was great. You sure told him.*

He grinned even more widely. "I didn't know you cared."

"I don't."

She couldn't handle those eyes sparkling at her, teasing her. She turned back to her drink and caught the bartender smiling, probably catching the word "naked" a few times. She pretended to look at the paraphernalia on the walls depicting all kinds of happy faces: buttons, posters, bottle caps, even round yellow faces with dreadlocks.

Her gaze fell to Chris's long fingers as they slid up and down the curves of his sweating bottle of beer. He had great hands, strong and capable, calloused and workworn. He tossed back the rest of his beer and set the bottle in front of him. The bartender brought another. He tipped it to her and took a swallow. He seemed different away from his dolphin. More relaxed, open.

He turned around on his stool and leaned back against the bar, one knee jiggling to the beat. His curls dipped to the top of his shirt in the back, and his biceps flexed as his arms balanced him. A few freckles topped his shoulders and that necklace lay over the curves of his collarbone. His tank top was deep blue, which brought out the green even more in his eyes. Did he have maps and beer and not much else wherever he lived?

She turned around, too, after waiting the appropriate amount of time so he didn't think she was copying him. She had to admit it was nice finding a familiar face among strangers. That was why she felt warm and easy sitting there with the fans pushing the air around and the music lulling her with its beat. Indeed, Barney's was a happy place.

"Where are you staying?" she asked, keeping her gaze just shy of his eyes.

"At The Caribe Plantation, down the road a piece."

She remembered seeing the fancy entrance earlier. It didn't seem like his style. "Sounds nice."

"The house is something, Colonial style with pillars and stuff. I'm staying in the boathouse."

That sounded more like Chris. When he didn't reciprocate, she said, "I'm staying at my father's apartment a few blocks from here."

He pulled one leg up and propped his chin on his knee. He leveled that gaze right at her, and she felt as though he were probing her mind. "So, Miz Lucy, what do you do back home?"

Even though she knew he was being sarcastic, something about the way he said her name felt the same way the music did as it washed over her in waves. "I own an advertising firm in St. Paul, Minnesota. Well, I own half of it. My ex-husband owns the other half, unfortunately."

He lifted his eyebrows, but not in the admiring way most people did when they heard she owned her own agency. "Ah, so you own a company that promotes greed, materialism and bodily perfection that most people can't live up to."

She didn't know what to say for a moment. "We get our client's product out there in the best light, the light that's going to appeal to people. And what appeals to people is—"

"Sex," he said, that light expression now gone from his face. "And excess."

"If that's what the client wants. We have some big clients, like Krugel. You know, the largest manufacturer of paper products in America...Soaker paper towels, Cloud Soft toilet paper." Her biggest client, and what did the lout have to say about it?

"So, you make your living telling people that if they wipe their tush with Cloud Soft, they'll be sexier."

It was so ridiculous, she almost laughed. Luckily she caught herself. "Forget about the toilet paper. We sell the company first, then their products. My company..." She narrowed her eyes at Chris. "Why do you make me feel like defending a profession I'm proud to be a part of?"

He shrugged. "Maybe somewhere deep inside, you aren't so proud of it."

"I beg to differ with you." Her shoulders stiffened. "I am very proud of my company and what we do. I've worked hard for my success."

He watched her, those eyes creating sensations that almost overruled her indignation. "What?" she asked at last.

"I was waiting to hear you beg." He swiveled around and grabbed his beer, which was already beaded with sweat.

"I don't beg for anything," she said at last, lifting her chin. She grabbed her glass and turned back to the open area. When she glanced his way, she was unsettled to find him watching her again. She was still stinging from his earlier comments, not to mention the begging remark. "I suppose you think you're some kind of hero, then. I mean, the irony of it—I push toilet paper and you save dolphins."

"Not at all." He took a sip of beer, scanning the crowd. "I put some of these dolphins where they are. It's my duty to get them out."

"What do you mean?" Despite his pigheadedness, she found herself wanting to know more about him.

"It's a long story," he said with a shrug.

"You've got a whole beer to go. Tell me."

He glanced at that beer as if it had betrayed him. "I worked at Aquatic Wonders down in the Keys for nine years. I started as the fish boy and worked my way up to head trainer, but in between, I also went out and caught wild dolphins for the park and to sell elsewhere. That was before I realized how unhappy they were in captivity, how wrong it was to keep them from their real home. Now I'm only trying to make up for my wrongs." He shrugged, as if it were all so inconsequential, though she knew by the look in his eyes that it wasn't. When he reached out and took hold of her wrist, she jerked responsively. "I hope your watch didn't get ruined when you fell in the pool."

His fingers felt cool and wet on her wrist. Because he was leaning close, she caught a whiff of shampoo and sea air. She glanced down at her diamond watch with the steamed face.

"I hadn't thought about it, actually." That watch had been her treat to herself the first year she made one-hundred-thousand dollars. But she wasn't about to tell him that. "I'm sure it'll be fine."

He wore the kind of watch that looked waterproof to about a thousand feet. "Or you can buy another one."

"Yes, I could do that, too."

"What kind of car do you drive?"

She found herself wanting to lie for some reason. "A BMW."

"I knew it."

"What do you know, mister almighty?"

"You're a status girl, aren't you?"

"What do you mean by that?"

"A Beemer, a diamond watch, you're probably wearing designer clothes and perfume, too. Probably even designer underwear," he added in a low, intimate voice that shivered through her.

As a matter of fact, she was, now that she thought about it. That's what she'd always worn, at least since her mother had married her wealthy stepfather.

"My underwear is none of your business. And so what if I am? What's it to you?"

He shook his head lazily. "It's nothing to me, Miz Lucy. Not a thing. Ah, you can't help it—you're another victim of the Great Green Lie."

"The what?" Why did it feel as though they spoke different languages?

"Green, money, the idea that money makes you happy, and the more you have the happier you are."

"I am happy." She wanted to shout it out, to somehow make him see how happy she was. "I am exactly where I want to be in my life. Not many people can say that when they're thirty. Can you?"

He lifted his chin in thought. "When I was thirty...let's see, I was in jail." He tipped back the rest of his beer and set it on the counter, then stood and pulled out some bills. "Have a nice vacation, Miz Lucy."

She watched him weave around the tables and out the front door, not a glance backward or a smile to soften his words. Her fingers clenched around the glass stem on her drink. She knew what he was trying to do: throw her off so she wouldn't talk to him the rest of her stay. And in case that didn't work, the jail thing might even scare her off.

Well, he didn't have to worry about that. She had no use for a man with an ocean-size chip on his shoulder.

She realized then that she'd come down here to eat, and he had distracted her. She ordered ribs and people-watched as she ate.

When the bartender brought her bill, she said, "My drink's not on here."

"Your man paid for your drink, miss." He shrugged, giving her a sympathetic look. "All that sex talk and begging, and he still leave. Maybe next time you should play coy." He batted his eyelashes.

She wanted to bat him. "If I need your advice, I'll ask for it, okay?"

He smiled. "No problem, mon."

She merely shook her head and slid off the barstool. This was not her night for men, and that was a fact.

3

THE BAHAMIAN SUN seemed even brighter and warmer than the one in St. Paul. Especially now that fall was moving in, rendering the air crisp and the skies muddy. But here in this strange world, the air was muggy and warm even at seven-thirty in the morning.

Lucy's heels clicked loudly across the concrete and echoed off the buildings as she made her way to the park's office. At lunch she would go shopping for something casual. She had resolved that under no circumstances would she even glance at Liberty's pool, but her gaze drew right to it. And right to Chris. All she could see of him was that head of curls and his shoulders gleaming in the early morning sun. Instantly she remembered his sultry words about seeing him naked. Worse, her body remembered, too, becoming hot and steamy itself. He wasn't serious. And just because he was sexy didn't mean she wanted to see him naked. As he started to glance up at the noise her shoes created, she averted her gaze to the wooden shutters of the office.

The air was warm and stale inside, without sign of an air conditioner anywhere. Just one old-fashioned fan that made the articles taped to the walls flutter. She propped the door open with a pink conch shell filled with cement. Once safely inside the office, she opened those shutters and peeked out over the other pools to Liberty.

"Good morning, Miss Lucy!" Bailey said in a loud, cheerful voice that made her jump.

Her fingers involuntarily slammed the shutters closed with a loud *clack*. She turned to his beaming face and tried not to look irritated, or worse, guilty.

"Good grief, Bailey, make some noise before coming in like that."

"Sorry, ma'am. I jus' wondered if you needed any help with the figures, or deciding on whether to keep the place open."

"No, but thank you. Being left alone will be the biggest help." She opened the shutters again, but did not look out. "I see the wicked man is back."

"Yah, in the wee hours this morning. I t'ink the man is part fish."

"That would explain a lot."

"Huh?"

"Nothing. All right, I've got to get to work."

It was easy to reduce her father's park to numbers. Business was her life, even if the creative side was her favorite part. Here, making it a business meant not looking at it as something her estranged father owned, and perhaps loved. Well, as much as a man like that could love something. He'd told her a few times that he'd loved her, too, but she felt neglected as perhaps Liberty was.

Silvery reflections from the Touching Tank danced across the walls like restless ghosts. Her gaze went out the window again, where Chris's long arms were outstretched and water splashed up to sparkle in the air. In some ways he reminded her of Sonny, or at least of the image she'd always had of him: seafaring, wandering and a loner. She wondered if he had ever been lonely, her father, and what he felt inside, and then she realized she was thinking about Chris and not her father at all.

"Hellooo," Bailey said in a singsong voice as he poked his head in the doorway a few hours later. "I didn't scare you dis time, did I?"

"Not much."

He stepped inside, looking crisp and professional in his white uniform. "Are you going to close us down?"

"I'm still looking at the numbers."

"I t'ink you were looking out da window, Miss Lucy," he said with a solemn nod.

She felt a warm flush and hoped he hadn't seen exactly where she'd been looking. "I was thinking. Now go away and let me think some more."

"Yes, Miss Lucy."

He disappeared, and she caught herself smiling. Miss Lucy. Her lips quirked even more. *Miz Lucy.* Chris only called her that in fun, but something in the way he said the words rippled through her. Ridiculous. Back to the numbers.

Not thirty minutes later, Bailey was back in the doorway with that white grin. "Decision yet?"

"No, and go away!"

BAILEY HELD OUT until almost noon this time.

She glanced over at her notepad full of numbers and calculations, then up at his hopeful face. "It doesn't look good." He dropped into one of the chairs in front of her desk. She felt as though she were firing the man, like she'd fired a few people back home. They looked the same way, and she felt the same way: bad. "This place was scraping by as it was. I don't know how long even Sonny could have kept it going. Without the star attraction, I don't see that it has a chance."

"We could buy another dolphin fish," he said.

"No, I'm afraid we can't afford one, no matter what

they cost. Besides, unless we get better facilities, Mr. Maddox will be back to take him away, too."

Bailey lifted an eyebrow. "You could beg him, you know, bat your eyelashes and say pretty please can we keep the dolphin fish?"

She lowered her chin. "Have you been talking to a particular bartender at Barney's?"

He looked innocent enough. "No, why?"

"Never mind. Anyway, I'm not the kind of woman who can convince a man to do things he doesn't want to do."

"Sure you are. You're very pretty."

"Thank you, but pretty isn't going to cut it. It never has, to be honest with you. Anyway, forget the begging thing. I'm not going to ask him to leave Liberty because I already know he won't."

"You're right," another voice said from the doorway. "You could be Marilyn Monroe reincarnated and you wouldn't get me to give Liberty back to you."

That flush Lucy experienced earlier was nothing compared to the full fire that lit her face now. She met those green eyes that reeked of smugness. "How long have you been standing there?"

"Since the begging thing."

She made a sound that combined embarrassment and irritation and wasn't ladylike by any means. "What do you want?"

Bailey made a quick exit, mumbling something about feeding the squid. Chris wore that bathing suit that had to be illegal on a body like his, moving up to her desk and planting his hands on the edge. His long fingers were shriveled underneath. He wore a band made of colored threads on his right wrist, though sun and water had faded it a little.

"I was wondering if Sonny kept any records on Liberty. Medical, training...anything like that."

If the person behind the desk was supposed to emit any kind of authority, she was doing a poor job. "You're dripping on my desk," she finally said, standing to face him.

He glanced down at the droplets of water swirling down his curls and puddling on the Formica surface. "Sorry." He stood, forcing her to look up at him again.

"I'll look around."

He glanced down at the paperwork scattered across the desk. "I can look if you're busy."

"I need a break anyway."

She found a junk drawer, another filled with more maps and notes on places like Aruba and Barbados, and stacks of *National Geographic* dating back to the seventies. She walked to the four-drawer filing cabinet. He walked up behind her, so close she could feel the moist heat emanating from him.

"Thanks for the drink, by the way," she said, diverting her thoughts.

"No problem."

Her fingers flipped through the hanging folders, nails clicking against the plastic tabs in Sonny's small writing that read Moray Eels, Sea Turtles and Clown Fish. It was then that she realized she hadn't only inherited numbers; she'd inherited living creatures that depended on humans to feed and take care of them. Who now depended on her.

"What's wrong?" he asked.

"There are so many creatures here."

"Haven't you seen them yet?"

She glanced to her left, finding him right beside her.

"Just a cursory glance. I wanted to look at the numbers first."

"Of course." He glanced back at the desk. "Did you inherit a moneymaker or a money pit?"

She turned to face him, finding him still too close to her personal zone. "I don't care about the money aspect. I just need to figure out what I'm going to do with this place."

"Surely not move here to run it, not the advertising princess."

She narrowed her eyes. "I am not an advertising princess."

He scanned her styled hair, gold-plated barrette, and continued slowly, agonizingly down the rest of her body. "Look like one to me." Despite his words, his eyes gave away some appreciation of what he saw.

The man was infuriating, but she tried her best to hold her mouth firm and not show him the effect his appraisal was having on her. She locked her knees and stood straighter. "Is there some reason you've chosen to pick on me? I mean, am I lucky, or are you holding my father's treatment of Liberty against me?"

"Neither."

"Okay, then for some reason you think I've, what, set my sights on you? That I'm attracted to you in some bizarre way, and you want to anger me so I'll change my mind?"

He chuckled softly, shaking his head. Leaning closer, he said, "Maybe I just enjoy getting your ire up." His hand slid past her and snatched a file from the drawer. "I'll return this when I'm done."

"Keep it!" she shouted after his glistening, retreating back.

Ooh, he was a wicked man.

LATER IN THE DAY, she took a cab into the shopping district to find appropriate attire. She felt out of place wearing tailored clothing among a population dressed for fun. Unfortunately, she was out of practice for fun.

Had she really thought that?

She was darn well going to get back into it, then. She bought several outfits, changing into white shorts and a flowery shirt before returning to the park.

The sight of Chris's moped made her smile and wince at the same time. He probably didn't even own a car, yet he could make fun of the car her friends, employees and most importantly, her ex, drooled over. What did the man know about being happy, anyway? The Great Green Lie, indeed.

She was surprised to find Chris absent from Liberty's pool, more surprised at feeling disappointed. Her leather sandals quietly took her over where Liberty swam in circles beneath the surface. She crouched down and watched him, pleased when he lifted his head out of the water to look at her. What secrets of the universe did he hold? Looking into that horseshoe-shaped pupil, she believed he knew them all.

"Hi there, fellow," she said, returning his grin.

She glanced around to see if Chris had left the bucket. "Sorry, guy, no fish to give you. I'm sure the creep will give you something soon."

She squeezed her eyes shut when she heard the creep walk up behind her. Not only had they gotten off on the wrong foot, they were walking a mile on it. Oh, but he was a gentleman as always. No snide remark from him, no rubbing in her tactless remark.

He simply threw a fish in her lap.

She screamed as the slimy, headless thing landed on

her, inadvertently batting it into the water where Liberty scooped it up. She jumped to her feet and faced Chris.

"You, you...."

"Creep?" he supplied with a lifted eyebrow.

"Yes!" She wiped at her new clothes, hoping they didn't smell of fish. "And a few other words I'm too much of a lady to use." No other man, even her ex, ruffled her the way Chris did.

He shrugged with one shoulder. "Sounded like you wanted to feed him, so I obliged. Shucks, I thought women liked chivalry."

She couldn't help the bark of laughter that escaped. "Chivalry? I'm surprised you even know the word. How many women do you know that like fish thrown at them? Tell me that, hmm?" She turned back to the dolphin, her hands still clenched at her sides. "And what is it around here with people sneaking up on me?"

Chris sat down at the edge of the pool, and Liberty seemed to know the bucket had arrived. He bobbed his head and made whistling, clicking noises. Chris lifted up his hand, and Liberty met his palm with a touch of his nose. Something tightened in Lucy's stomach at that simple act of trust.

"Aw, that is so sweet, touching his nose to your hand."

He broke the moment by pointing out, "That's not his nose. His nose is here." He gestured to Liberty's blowhole. "That's where he breathes. He touched my hand with his snout."

"I'm just learning more and more each day." Despite the teacher, she did want to know more about Liberty.

"I'd ask if you wanted to feed him, but I know the advertising princess wouldn't want to touch a dead fish."

She narrowed her eyes at him. "Give me the stupid

fish." Why was it so important to prove him wrong? "And this time not in my lap, *if* you don't mind."

"Come to think of it, I didn't get very high scores in chivalry class." He handed her a Spanish mackerel, trying not to laugh as she took it with the very tips of her polished fingernails. He was goading her and enjoying the heck out of it. What he wasn't sure of was exactly why he was doing either.

"Hold it beneath the water," he said. "I'm trying to get him to eat underwater from now on, like wild dolphins do."

She dangled the fish by where the tail used to be, and Liberty lifted himself up out of the water. "No, no, you have to let me put it in the water," she said earnestly, all traces of her ire gone. She dunked the fish in the water, and Liberty took hold of it. Her delight caught him in the gut, a look of pure amazement on a heart-shaped face that was prettier than she thought. Not Marilyn Monroe pretty, but pretty enough.

Liberty came out of the water and tossed the fish to position it before swallowing it. Lucy giggled, then turned to him. "Can I feed him again?"

He should have told her to scram. He had work to do and he wanted as little human contact with Liberty as possible. But before he could form those words, his hand was already passing her another mackerel.

"Why don't you just free him now?" she asked.

"Because he's not used to fending for himself." He threw another fish to the far side of the pool. "He's been humanized. Everything a dolphin is comes from his hierarchy within the pod."

"You mentioned a pod before. What exactly is it?"

"The school or any group of dolphins. Together, they can protect each other and hunt for food. Liberty here is a nobody. He probably doesn't even know he's a dolphin anymore."

She watched Liberty with such compassion, he was actually touched for a moment. Then he remembered who she was, what she represented.

"I have to teach him to become a dolphin, to catch live fish, and to swim in a straight line again. It's not only Liberty's health I want to restore, it's his spirit."

She looked at him with those deep brown eyes. "I think that's...wonderful."

He looked away, uncomfortable with that gaze. "It's just what I do."

"Do you get paid for doing this?"

He laughed, because that sounded more like the advertising princess. "Untraining dolphins is not on the list of professions a woman looks for in a future husband. In other words," he said before she could get too huffy, "no, I don't get paid. Someone usually contacts me about a dolphin in trouble, and I ask them to get someone to sponsor me to come out and investigate. I get proof and go to the authorities for permission to free the dolphin. People send in donations, and when I'm home, I work odd jobs to get by."

Liberty swam by, brushing against his legs. Contact, trust. It was a start. He put his hand into the water, but Liberty hesitated, keeping his distance.

"So you travel all over doing this?" she asked.

"Yep."

"Why?"

He stood, less comfortable with her questions than with her gaze. "Like I said, it's what I do."

She stood too, planting her hands on her hips. "You should hire an agency to get the word out about your organization and bring in financial support."

He laughed, shaking his head. "Yeah, right. I can't afford any kind of agency, and I don't want what I do played out to tug at the heartstrings of America. I do the occasional radio or television appearance because it's good for publicity, and that's it."

"Fine, whatever," she said in clipped tones.

She'd changed into clothing more befitting to the atmosphere, but he wasn't about to comment on that or her nice legs in those blue shorts. Or the way the red hibiscus flowers on her shirt molded to her full breasts in the breeze. He didn't want the advertising princess to get the wrong idea. She was definitely not his speed. He was in the no-wake zone, she was freeway.

"So, Miz Lucy, what are you going to do with this place anyway?"

She looked around, as if the answer might be found somewhere nearby. Bailey waved, his smile overly bright.

"Do you really care, now that you have your dolphin?"

He shrugged. "I'm wondering more for all of the other marine animals. If you sell it to someone like your father, what will happen to everything in here?"

She looked at him, her brows furrowed. "You don't think my father mistreated Liberty because he was... wicked, do you?"

"No," he said with some amount of certainty. She obviously wanted to believe her father wasn't such a bad guy; he could grant her that. "He was looking at the bottom line. And he probably just didn't know any better. Mostly, people think animals are put here for our amusement or use. He was one of those people." He turned back to the pool, more comfortable with working with the dolphin than talking to Lucy. "Well, Miz Lucy, if you don't mind, I have work to do." He tipped his head at her and slid into the water.

He waited a few minutes before looking back to see her walking to the long building that housed the aquariums. She didn't know her father, wasn't aware that he even owned this place if he remembered correctly. But she'd done all right anyway, at least by the world's standards. And she definitely belonged in that world. He'd be glad when she returned to it. She was fast becoming a temptation he didn't need.

4

LUCY WONDERED if Chris had been born a creep or had become one somewhere along the way. What had happened to create his disdain of people? What she really wanted to know was why she even bothered to wonder. She wandered into the cavernous aquarium building.

He could scoff all he wanted, but having a great job, being her own boss, owning a nice apartment and being able to buy virtually whatever she wanted constituted a great life, one that most people wanted. And a guy who had nothing was making her feel defensive about it, calling it, what? The Great Green Lie. Jerk. Her life was perfect. Okay, maybe she could use a man in it. Probably she should just get a dog.

Bailey was nearby, explaining the mating habits of the octopus to some tourists. He was a nice guy, but she couldn't keep the place open for him and Bill, could she? No, but she could give them good severance packages, references, that kind of thing.

Bailey demonstrated with his fingers as he spoke. "Dey wrap their tenta-clees around each other like dis, and become one big ball of legs. Den dey roll around on the ocean floor, sometimes for days at a time." She shot him a questioning look, and he added, "Okay, maybe not days, but certainly hours."

Oh, brother. She was no expert on the mating habits of the octopus, barely even knew the mating habits of humans anymore. But something about Bailey's story, like his family, didn't sound quite right.

She walked past the tanks, entranced by all the creatures that normally lived in the ocean beyond: brightly colored fish, crabs, even a jewfish. What were their lives like in the wild? She thought of Chris's question about what she would do with the park. At the moment, she felt responsible for the lives of the lobsters, eels, all of them. Some did the same thing Liberty did, circling endlessly in their small, boring worlds. All for the amusement of tourists.

She sighed, overwhelmed by what was right. Still, she couldn't imagine spending her life trying to save any one of these species. That was for someone who had different values, different standards to live by. Like Chris.

"Well, Miss Lucy, did you convince him to let da dolphin fish stay?" Bailey asked, coming up beside her.

"I want the dolphin to go free, Bailey. It's only right."

"Kiss mi neck, I t'ink you *are* sweet on the guy!"

She whirled around, mouth open. "Bailey! Why in the world would you think I was sweet on that...creep?"

"The way you look at him all the time, and the way you took his side."

"I didn't take his side, I took the dolphin's side."

He didn't look convinced.

"And speaking of creeps," she said, "I have to call my ex and see how everything's going."

She walked toward the office. Sweet on him! Of all the crazy, harebrained ideas. She was as sweet on Chris as she was on the pukey green moray eel in one of the tanks. Chris and the eel had about the same amount of charm, to be sure.

First, she touched base with her secretary, then she was transferred to Tom.

"Hey, how come you're not checking your e-mail?" he said.

"I'm just fine, and yourself?"

"What, I'm supposed to deal with pleasantries when you've been totally out of reach for the past week?"

"It's only been a day and a half, and dispensing with the pleasantries was the reason our marriage disintegrated, so keep that in mind when you're out with that little honey I saw you with last weekend."

He chuckled, and she could well imagine that cocky grin of his. "Aw, you're just jealous."

All she could do was laugh. "Would I be giving you *advice* if I were jealous?"

"Well, I suppose not. But you didn't have to laugh."

"Sorry, couldn't help it."

"Anyway, why haven't you checked your e-mail?"

"Because I didn't bring my laptop with me. I told you this was also a vacation."

"That's what I say when I leave town, too, but I'm still right there in the groove, Luce."

She ground her teeth together. "Are you saying I'm not pulling my load?" It wasn't the first time she'd asked that question, but Tom was too much of a wimp to say what he occasionally alluded to. "Because if you are, we can talk about dissolving Advertising Genius when I get back. Frankly, I'm tired of your innuendoes."

She could hear him put his smile in place. "No, darling, I'm only...all right, sometimes I do feel that way, but I don't want to dissolve. It's just that, when we were married we both put everything into the business. I still am, and you're not."

"That's why we're not married anymore, Tom. Our marriage was the business. That's all it was. I am totally committed to the agency, but I really need this time away. And don't call me darling. I haven't been your darling for a long, long time. So, what is this emergency you've been trying to get hold of me over?"

"No emergency, Luce, I only wanted to make sure you were accessible if one arose."

She blew out a long breath. "Well, I'm not accessible. In fact, I haven't even thought of the agency since I left." She realized that was true, except for the brief but irritating conversation with Chris last night. "And I don't feel bad about it. I'm allowed to do that, take a real vacation, you know."

"Have you got that tropical fever? Maybe you'd better come right back and see a doctor. You want me to make the arrangements?"

"I do not have any tropical fever. It's just that I have enough to deal with right here, and I want this settled before I return."

Tom had a way of sounding like a boy at times, and that tone crept into his voice now. "So, what's that park you inherited like? Primitive little place?"

Ever since he'd heard about her inheritance, he'd been sniveling about it. "No, it's great, huge, with dolphin shows and a hundred aquariums filled with exotic marine animals, and you should see the crowds. It's right on the ocean, a real gold mine."

And then she turned to find Chris standing there with that folder in his hand.

"That sounds…nice. Hey, my line is blinking, and I have a meeting with a big, prospective client in twenty minutes. Will you call in once a day at least?"

"I will not. I may call in a few days, but I'm not making any promises. Bye."

She laughed nervously when she hung up. "I can explain that little…exaggeration."

Chris shook his head. "Listen, I gave up on trying to understand people a long time ago."

"This is different."

He replaced the green folder.

"See, that was my ex, the one I own the agency with, and he makes me so crazy sometimes with his attitude, and I don't even know why I lied."

He snagged her hands, which were trying to express what she was saying. "I don't care. It's all part of the Great Green Lie, and that's not my world anymore."

He glanced down to where he held her hands. She wondered if it felt as good to him as it did to her. As though in answer, he tightened his hold before releasing her and heading out. She curled her fist and tapped her forehead with it. What a fool she'd made of herself! Not only caught in an inane lie, but babbling to try to explain it. She hated what Tom made her sometimes. But it wasn't just Tom, it was everything.

It was who she was.

BY THE END of the day, Lucy had contacted a real-estate person to come out and give her an idea of what the property was worth. She tried to find Bailey to tell him she was leaving, but found herself at Liberty's pool where Bailey was nowhere near.

Chris was floating on a blue raft, arms and feet dangling in the water. He was still wearing that swimsuit that accentuated his small derriere and the taper of his back as it flared into nice, wide shoulders. She caught herself licking her lips. It wasn't like her to lust, other than at untouchable celebrities. Chris was definitely touchable, at least in a physical sense. Liberty swam below him, like an odd-shaped shadow.

"You're not going to try to explain yourself again, are you?" he said.

"I don't care what you think."

His lips quirked. "Yeah, right. You even cared that a bartender thought you'd seen me naked. What do you want? I'm busy."

She tried to let his rudeness roll off her, but it stuck in her skin like a cactus spine instead. "You don't look very busy."

"I'm observing him. I want him to get used to my being here without thinking he has to react to me. I don't want him to think of me as human so much as just something in his area."

"Like a piece of seaweed?" She couldn't help the grin that erupted on her face as he lifted an eyebrow at the comparison. *Wonder what he'd think about the eel comparison?* Their gazes held until she had to clear her throat and focus on the dolphin again. "I wouldn't think he'd like humans very much."

"Would you blame him?" He rolled over on his side, facing her. "But they hold no grudges. They actually seem to like people, though I can't understand why."

She looked at him, wondering again what made him dislike people so much. "He seems to like you, though I can't understand why." He splashed water at her. She ducked, but caught the edge of the spray. "Ah, you can dish it out, but you can't take it, eh?"

He laced his fingers behind his head. "Come here and I'll show you how I can take it."

"Uh-uh. I've already had a fish thrown in my lap and now a saltwater bath. I think I'll pass." She waved dismissively at him and turned to go, but her heart had somehow taken off in some other direction because it was thumping heavily inside her. *Good grief, he was just goading you on, girl. Don't be a fool.*

LUCY FINISHED packing up the apartment of the man who had fathered her. She put the maps in a separate box, not exactly sure what she was going to do with them. Her mother thought she was crazy for coming down to this "tropical infestation of drugs and bugs," but Lucy was glad she'd come. This gave her a sense of closure she'd never had concerning her birth father.

Her mother called Sonny a bum, a loser, and she'd wanted that influence nowhere near her daughter. Lucy knew her mother hadn't made it easy for Sonny to keep in touch, but she still wished he had. Maybe he had been a bum in some ways, but he'd been her father. She decided that she was proud to call him that.

She flicked on the small television to watch the weather. It still amazed her that she hadn't thought about work, much less home, since she'd left.

Cold and rainy in St. Paul. Time to call her best friend Vicki and rub it in. Vicki was a journalist for one of the large St. Paul newspapers. They'd met years ago when Vicki did a piece on Advertising Genius, and they'd been friends ever since. She dialed the number, waiting to hear Vicki's always-cheerful voice. Sometimes Lucy wished she could be more like her friend, spontaneous and care-free. Lucy couldn't remember ever being that way, even when she was little. *Be a good girl, Lucy. Act like a proper lady now.*

"Hello!" Vicki answered breathlessly.

"Hi, it's me."

"Lucy! It's about time! Hold on, let me get my portable phone. I just walked in." After a second, she said, "I'm looking at a picture from a magazine of the Bahamas

with beaches as white as snow and water the color of
glass cleaner that can't be real. So...is it beautiful there?"

Lucy bit her lower lip as the image of Chris flashed
through her mind. "Actually, I haven't had a chance to
look at the beach." And the water was right there beyond
the park's boundaries.

"Oh, Lucy, that is so like you! This is supposed to be a
vacation, isn't it?"

"Yes and no. But it's more complicated than that. I
have to decide what to do with the park. And there's this
guy who's taken custody of the dolphin there and is
training—or rather untraining him to set him free."

"A guy?" She could see Vicki's blond eyebrows shoot-
ing up in interest.

"Yes, a guy. Anyway, I've been busy—"

"What about the guy?"

"He's not that kind of a guy."

"What is he, then?"

"What I mean is, it's not like that. Don't romanticize it,
please." Lucy laughed at the concept. "He and I barely
get along."

"Is he cute?"

"Mmm, yeah, I'd say that. Tall, blond curly hair, thin
but muscular, and these green eyes that—he's okay."

"Lucy," Vicki said, drawing out her name. "You're
holding out on me."

Lucy looked around, paranoid that somehow someone
would be standing there. "This is going to sound like a
romance novel, but when I look at his eyes, it's like I'm
falling in. All right, he's gorgeous, but that's all there is to
it. He spends his days saving dolphins. I mean, that's his
job. Sort of, because he doesn't get paid for it. But he says
he's not a hero, and I believe he does feel that way."

"I still think you're holding out on me."

"He and I got off on the wrong foot, and we've been stumbling ever since. He doesn't even like people, and he calls me the advertising princess." She smiled. "And Miz Lucy."

Vicki was making swooning noises on the other end of the phone. When she finally composed herself, she said, "Oh, man, he sounds delicious! And I know he is, because I can hear that little smile in your voice."

"You cannot," Lucy said, trying to scrunch her mouth into a straight line.

"Yes, I can," Vicki teased. "All right, so *what*—he's not your type, which in my opinion is boring if Tom is any indication and that's about all the indication I have to go on because I think you've dated what, once, maybe twice, counting that bozo from Michigan, so maybe not-your-type is exactly your type. Have you thought of that?"

Lucy raised her eyebrows, trying to assimilate that last statement. "You think my type is boring?"

"Yes. Come on, Lucy, you go for the got-it-together suit, drives a fancy import and has a respectable, stable job. Maybe it'll be good for you to, you know, have a fling with this guy. An island romance!"

"A *fling*? You're suggesting I have a fling?"

"Yep. You need to loosen up. And what better way to do it than with this dolphin guy with the—did you say *blond curls*? Ooooh, I love blond curls!"

"Well, they're sort of golden, actually—" She caught herself twirling her hair and stopped. "Vicki, forget it. You know I'm too sensible for a fling."

"That's your problem. You're too sensible, too good, too smart. Throw it all away for a change."

"You're a bad influence on me, you know that? But it's not going to work. For one thing, this guy can't stand me.

He thinks I'm materialistic, ambitious, too caught up in success."

"Well, you are."

"What's wrong with that? Look at what I have because of who I am."

"I know, girl, but there's more to life than designer clothes and fancy wheels."

"No, there isn't. Besides, I could never live with myself if I slept with this guy and never saw him again."

Vicki laughed. "Happens all the time. Okay, so bring him back with you."

Now it was Lucy's turn to laugh. "Does the term *fish out of water* mean anything to you? This guy is a fish. Or maybe part dolphin. I can't even imagine him in my world." She tried to picture him at a cocktail party, wearing his tiny trunks and the shark's-tooth necklace. And Tom's face when he met Chris, which made her laugh out loud again. "No, it would never work. Besides, didn't you hear me? He can't stand me. He threw a fish at me today."

"That's always a sign that they like you."

"In what country? But he did let me feed the dolphin. Liberty is so cool, and he pressed his nose—snout right up to Chris's hand, and aw, you should have seen it."

"Chris is the guy, I hope, and Liberty the dolphin?"

"Yes, Chris is the guy." She cleared that ridiculous dreamy sound from her voice. "The pain in the neck. So, what do you want me to bring you back?"

"Okay, here's what I want: I want a picture of this Chris guy. And a picture of that beach so I can compare and make sure this ad agency didn't enhance the photograph. And I want you to come back with an I've-been-thoroughly-loved-up-one-side-and-down-the-other look on your face."

"Bye, Vicki."

"Bye, Lucy. And I mean it about the look!"

She shook her head as she hung up the phone. "Vicki, I'm thinking that I don't want to be like you at this moment. Shame on you. I've never told you I wanted to be like you so I can't tell you that I don't. In fact, you're the one always saying how I have it together, how you envy that. But I never told you about the empty ache inside."

5

LUCY MADE A POINT that morning to check out the color of the ocean beyond the park, but the skies were overcast. Whitecaps tipped the grayish water, and a distant rumble echoed off the building behind her.

Another sound rumbled through her—splashing water and Chris's low, coaxing voice.

"That's it. Oh, yeah. Perfect."

Those words slinked through her body in a way that she could not, did not, want to explain. When Vicki's words about having a fling drifted through her mind, the hot, rapid response of her body made Lucy more resolute in avoiding Chris.

Then she heard a trill, happy chattering that drew her attention to Liberty. His head bobbed up and down, and to Lucy's surprise, he was looking at her. She felt touched and warm and a little giddy all at once.

"Well, isn't that just like a guy?" Chris said. "A pretty woman throws him a fish, and now he's smitten."

The compliment—or at least she thought it was a compliment—swirled through her, riding on the edge of that low voice. She walked over and crouched by the edge of the pool. At first Liberty swam away from her, making her wonder if she'd moved in too fast. With his bruised snout, he balanced an inflatable striped ball as he made his way back to her. He tossed it to her, and for a moment, all she could do was stare at him.

"He wants you to throw it back," Chris said, pulling himself up on the opposite edge of the pool.

Sheets of water poured off his body, and she forced herself to focus on his eyes instead. When she couldn't see anything disapproving, she tossed the ball out, and Liberty batted it back to her. The next time he hit the ball toward Chris, and so the game went, first to Lucy, then to Chris. She couldn't stop grinning.

When Liberty tired of the game, he positioned himself for his treat. Chris merely shook his head. Only when Liberty gave up and ducked beneath the water did Chris throw a fish. Lucy never thought feeding an animal could be so exciting, but there was something about feeding Liberty the day before that still touched her. Because he trusted her, maybe. Because they were from different worlds and should never have even met. She found her gaze had moved to Chris where she found those green eyes watching her.

"Do you want to feed him?" he asked.

"Yes." She smiled, feeling shy all of a sudden. Shy? Good grief, when was the last time she'd felt like that?

He tossed one of those mackerels her way, but Liberty leaped up midway and snatched it out of the air. After splashing back down into the water, he raised his head and bobbed it.

"You're welcome," she said with a laugh, wiping water from her face. "You've come a long way with him since yesterday."

That gaze held her, pinned her to the spot and to that breath. "He's lonely."

She nodded slowly. "I imagine he is."

"Lonely enough to even want the company of humans," he added, breaking that spell with the hard tone underlying his voice.

She found herself wanting to ask if he felt the same way, but thank goodness he glanced back toward the office before she could make an idiot of herself.

"Looks like you have company, Miz Lucy."

Bailey was bringing over a man perhaps a few years older than she, wearing a flowery silk shirt and baggy pants that both flapped in the breeze. He finger-combed his straight, slick blond locks, which immediately blew into disarray again. Banks of gray clouds sailed over them, darkening everything in their path including the man whose hand was already extended and aimed right at her, along with a dynamic smile.

"Ms. Donovan," he said with a slight British accent, squeezing her hand in a tight hold and wrenching it up and down. "I'm Crandall Morton with the Caribbean Real Estate Group. A pleasure to meet you, and might I say how much I appreciate your calling us."

"Nice to meet you," Lucy said. Now this man was a gentleman. Maybe Chris could pick up a few pointers. "And this is—" She turned to introduce the Bohemian, but he was already back in the pool with the dolphin.

"The dolphin fish, er, tief?" Crandall said, glancing toward Bailey to indicate where he'd gotten the expression.

"Ah, never mind him. Let's go to the office, shall we?"

She found it refreshing to talk to a civilized man about numbers and business. So why did she decline his dinner invitation by making up some excuse about packing up her father's things when that was already done?

"Perhaps another night before you leave?" he asked, a gracious smile on his thin lips.

"Perhaps," she said, walking him to the front gate.

He stepped into one of the nicer cars she'd seen on the island and waved as he drove away. If she were to have a fling—which she wouldn't—that man would be more her type. Successful, classy men were her style. Not dripping-wet-watching-the-sky-darken-wearing-those-little-trunks-again-who-liked-to-ignore-her types.

And if not, why was she invariably walking his way? Luckily Bailey intercepted her.

"You not going to sell dis place to dat guy, are you?"

"Why not? He represents an investor who's going to put a charming hotel on this property, which is worth more as land than it is as a park."

Bailey scowled. "He came in talking to Sonny about dat."

"Crandall mentioned he'd talked to Sonny."

"Sonny hate the guy. He always come round trying to badger Sonny into selling the park to put up some high-rise condominiums. Sonny, he love dis park."

She wasn't sure if Bailey was a reliable source on anything. One of them was lying about the relationship between her father and Crandall, and she'd bet on Bailey first. But she grasped onto the last part of what he'd said.

"My father loved this place?"

"Yah, mon. It mean the world to him."

Her gaze swept from one end of the park, pausing at Chris, to the other. The aquarium needed painting, the office needed refurbishing and most of the signs were faded.

"He had a strange way of treating what he loved," she said.

"He love you, too, Miss Lucy. He used to watch the kids, especially girls wit' brown hair, and get dis sad smile on his face."

She turned to Bailey. "I didn't mean—"

"I know what you mean. He used to talk about you, you know."

Her voice grew small when she asked, "He did?"

He nodded. "He tell everyone what a big shot his girl is, how proud he was."

She chewed on her bottom lip, sure that the moisture gathering in her eyes was due to the spray of salty mist a gust of wind blew up from the ocean.

Bailey scanned the sky. "I don' t'ink we gonna have much business today. Tropical storm gonna be here all day, and the cruise ships no going to send people ashore on ferries when it's rough."

A bank of dark clouds shimmered with electricity in the distance, and shades of gray mottled the entire sky. The wind was having a heyday with Chris's curls as he slipped into a white cotton shirt and red shorts.

She forced herself to turn to Bailey. "What did Sonny do on days like this?"

"If the weather was going to be bad all day, he jus' close up. Everyt'ing's been fed, except for the ones who get fed during the tours."

She could see one of the cruise ships in the distance rising and falling on the swells. It looked like a toy ship in a child's tub. "All right, let's close."

"Yes!" Bailey said with jerk of his fist. "Not'ing like snuggling up with the one you love on a day like dis. I'll feed the sharks and stingrays and go right away."

"The one you love would be the mother of your six children, I hope!" she called after him, but he was already sprinting toward the aquarium.

"He's got six kids?" Chris asked from her side.

"It depends on when you ask him. It's a variation of kids and goats."

He rubbed a towel over his curls and then gave them a shake. "You closing down for the day?"

She glanced around at the banners being whipped in

the wind, at Bailey tossing food in the pools. "No point in staying open."

"Not unless you want to get struck by lightning. I'm off to Barney's. See ya."

He headed for the front gate, and she turned back to the office. Bailey jogged through the gate at the same time Bill turned the sign around and headed to his car.

Suddenly a whole day stretched out before her with nothing to fill it. Hanging around in the office didn't sound appealing, nor did hanging around her father's apartment. When she turned back to Chris, he was standing a few yards away looking at her.

"I don't suppose you'd want to wait out the storm at Barney's with me."

Her mouth quirked in a half smile. "Is that supposed to be an invitation?"

He seemed to consider that. "Yeah, I guess it is."

"Well, then, I guess I'll accept."

He nodded toward the moped. "We'd better get going before the rain starts."

"Oh, no, I'm not getting on one of those things."

A teasing glint lit his eyes. "Miz Lucy, I'll bet you've never done anything daring in your life, have you?"

"I most certainly have. I started a business right out of college. That was risky. I came down here by myself."

"Ooh, paint me wrong. Come on, let's go. It'll be pouring by the time a cab comes."

She found herself following him outside the gate, which she locked. He was already starting the engine. She stared at him, with his shirt flapping open and his long legs bracing the bike. This was dangerous, insane. Risky? Probably. She glanced behind her, watching the squall thunder in.

Straightening her shoulders, she stepped forward and

tried to remember how she'd seen other women ride motorcycles. Chris scooted forward on the small seat, and she tried to sit down without getting too close to him.

"Ready?" he called over the wind and the engine.

She took a quick breath. "I suppose so. I mean, yes, I'm ready."

"You'd better put your arms around me so you don't fall off."

She looked at his broad back. "Hold on where exactly?"

"I'll demonstrate." And then he hit the gas.

With a yelp, she grabbed on to his shoulders, sliding forward on the seat until they were pressed together more intimately than she'd wanted. "You...you..."

"I believe creep was your word of choice."

"Yes! That's the nicest word I can think of."

"It worked, didn't it? You go with your instinct."

But when he took a corner, her fingers started sliding down his shirt. She lowered her hands to his waist, which was thinner and more graspable. When they hit a pothole in the road, her arms automatically went around him. Now her chest was pressed against his back, and her body started at the feel of his warmth and solidity. Geez, she hadn't been this physically close to a man in...she shook her head, not wanting to know exactly.

"You all right back there?" he asked.

"Fine," she murmured, laying her cheek against him as well. The sight of the road and cars flashing by made her dizzy. With every jarring hole or dip in the road, she pressed closer. The engine vibrated through her, and she closed her eyes and lost herself in the feel of the air that was cool and the warmth that emanated between their bodies. A strange and wonderful sensation curled through her, and she pressed her pelvis against him.

Pure, sensual pleasure poured through her. She felt a long, deep breath rumble inside and release on the wind as something close to a sigh. And then her eyes snapped open and she sat up straighter.

"Oh, *gawd!*"

"What's wrong?" he asked.

"I forgot about driving on the left side. It sort of startled me."

She shook her head. Yeah, right. How utterly embarrassing. How long had it really been?

He leaned his head back. "Why are you blushing?"

"I am *not* blushing, and please keep your eyes on the road. We are, like, totally out in the open here where everyone can see...I mean, hit us." Oh, no, what had she *looked* like, speeding down the street snuggled up against him? He was looking at her again. "Watch the road!"

When she slid her arms back around him, she felt his bare flesh beneath the flapping shirt. She decided to keep them there instead of appearing to be prudish and pulling the shirt down. His skin was warm and soft, all hard muscle beneath. She would not lose herself in the feel of him again. She would not—

When she glanced to the right, she saw Barney's go flying by.

"We passed Barney's!" she said.

"Hold on."

As he slowed down, her fingers reflexively tightened against him, and her body pressed closer as they leaned into the turn-around.

"You must have gotten caught up in the scenery, too," she said, trying to inject a laugh in her voice.

"Without a doubt."

They pulled in just as the rain began to dump down. They were both drenched when they walked inside, and she couldn't help laughing as the eight or so people in the bar looked up at them.

"Come on in, mon," a different bartender called to them. "We're having a warm-up-dry-down special jus' now. It's called a Rasta Runner, and I guarantee it will heat your blood up."

Lucy did not need her blood heated again. "I'll just have a soda."

"Red Stripe for me," Chris called, heading over to a table near the outer edge of the place.

The exterior half walls allowed the rain-drenched air to seep in and cool everything down. She followed him, stopping short when he took off his shirt, held it out the window, and twisted the water out of it. She pulled at hers, but it stuck back to her skin again.

"It's not fair that men can do that," she said, sitting down and propping her feet up on the chair across from hers.

He turned to her as he shook out his shirt and hung it on the back of the chair. "Go right ahead."

She wrinkled her nose at him. "Not today."

She watched him walk to the bar to pick up their drinks. He had the easy gait of a man who was comfortable with himself. When he set down her soda in front of her, he leaned forward and brushed a strand of hair from her cheek. It was a casual movement, yet she froze for a moment when his finger touched her skin.

"You had a hair..." He gestured vaguely toward his face, then dug in his pocket and took out a couple of quarters. "I'm going to play some music. This place doesn't seem the same without tunes."

She jumped up. "Let me. Please."

He handed her the coins, and she made her way to the

jukebox. Jimmy was already singing "Margaritaville" by the time she got back to the table.

"I never would have figured you for a parrothead," he said, propping his sandal-clad feet up on the sill.

"A what?"

"Parrothead. That's what they call Buffett fans."

She smiled, pulling her knee up and resting her chin on it. "I wouldn't consider myself a...parrothead. But I like this music. It kind of reminds me of..." She shook her head. "Nothing."

"Reminds you of what?"

She never talked to anyone about this. "It's kind of silly."

He didn't have to say a word, but urged her on by the way he waited.

"Well, I didn't really know my father when I was growing up. All I knew about him was that he sailed around the Bahamas and never settled down or got a good job, which is why my mother divorced him. So I kind of got this image of him, sailing the seven seas, maybe even with a patch over his eye. When I hear this music, I think of him just that way." Her smile faded when she met his gaze. "I told you it's silly."

"That's not silly." He took a sip of his beer. "You said you didn't know he had a park down here."

"Nope. Found out from the lawyer. I never heard from him all that much. Mother didn't exactly make it easy for him to see me." She cleared the haziness from her voice, looking out at the wall of rain beyond the window. A gust of cool, damp air ruffled the napkins on the table. "Let's talk about you."

"Let's not talk about anything."

"But you must have such an exciting life, saving the dolphins and all."

"My life is great. Perfect. I travel all over the country, usually beautiful, tropical, sunny places like this." He lifted his hand toward the window, and they both laughed. "And I like what I do."

"But you don't make much money at it. And you're never home."

"I have a place down in the Keys, a small place on the water. But I don't like staying in one spot too long. And I don't care about the money."

She sat up straight. "How can you not care about money? I mean, we all have to have it to live and survive. It makes life comfortable. It gives you things that make you happy."

He leaned toward the rough table surface, balancing his chin on his fingers. "Does your Beemer and all that other stuff make you happy, Miz Lucy?"

"Of course it does. Very. I like getting in my nice car and smelling the leather and going fast. I like being able to buy whatever I want. I like having a regular schedule, getting up in the morning and knowing I have a job to go to." She wasn't about to tell him about that empty spot inside her.

He leaned back in his chair. "Okay."

"Okay?"

"If you say so."

"I do. I can't imagine what I would do if I didn't have my goals."

"As long as you're happy."

"Very happy. Ecstatically happy."

"Then why were you lying about the park?"

"I thought you didn't want me to explain." He shrugged, but waited for her answer. "It's stupid, I know. It's the competition thing. We've always been that way, even when we were dating. And before Tom, it was my two stepsisters. Our parents encouraged us to compete, to be the best we could be and better than anyone else."

"I'm sure you've made them very proud."

She couldn't tell whether he was patronizing her or not. He wasn't easy to read like her ex-husband was. "They are." She didn't want to talk about her happiness anymore. Her very ecstatic happiness. "And you're happy?"

"Yes."

"That's it? Not very, wonderfully or anything else?"

"Nope, just happy."

And he was. He didn't have to go on like she did, defending her happiness to the bitter end. "What made you like dolphins more than people? Why don't you like to stay in one place too long?"

"Because I'm a quiet, private person who doesn't like people asking a lot of questions."

"But why..." Her voice broke off as she realized what he'd implied. *Lucy, admit it: you're dying to know more about him. Well, yes, but only out of...curiosity. Nothing more.* "Can you at least tell me why you went to jail?"

He lifted an eyebrow at her, though his lips were tinged in a smile. "You don't give up, do you?"

She trailed her finger in the condensation of her bottle of cola. "I want to know if you're a mass murderer or something." She shrugged. "Just for the record."

"You want the gory version or the nice version?"

She tapped the side of her bottle, contemplating. "I'd better hear the gory version."

He got up and walked over to the bar with his empty bottle. The rain had lightened considerably, leaving a solid slate-colored sky behind. She could hear the waves lapping against the shore. What kind of vacation was this, anyway? Spending her time cooped up in an office deciding the fate of several hundred sea specimens and one Bailey and one Bill, hanging around a man who enjoyed ignoring her, or merely irritating her, and not soaking in any of the beauty around her. *Hmph.*

Then she realized she was staring at his backside, from the way his damp curls brushed against his back of his neck, the expanse of tan, muscular back that tapered to his shorts. She felt a tingle start in her chest and travel languidly to more southern regions. Instead of feeling annoyed about that, she let herself enjoy it. See, she was soaking in some local beauty. Vicki's words about having a fling floated through her mind, upping the tantalization level—until she realized it wasn't Vicki's voice urging her on. It was her own.

Chris walked back over, a Red Stripe in one hand and a bottle of Ting in the other. "Let's go for a walk." He headed out the back door leading to the beach.

She sat there for a moment, though her body strained to jump up and follow him. Lucy Donovan did not follow. She did not let some good-looking man lead her around on a leash for his enjoyment. She might get up at her own pace and leisurely stroll out the same door he happened to stroll out, and might possibly join him if he was going in the same direction she happened to be going in. She spotted him standing several yards to the left and decided that might be a good direction to take.

"You were telling me about the time you went to jail. The gory version."

He slid her a sideways glance. "I was, huh?"

"Yep."

The damp sand crept into her sandals and between her toes. Although it was early afternoon, it felt more like evening. The gray sky tainted the ocean with the same dull color. People were starting to come back out again, but the wide, beige beach was still fairly deserted.

He headed to a large cement structure that jutted out into the water. It seemed to have no particular purpose, no markings or railing. He walked a few feet ahead of her, drawn to the water like a fish. His hair was still damp and mussed, his chest bare and tan. He looked wild and reckless and careless, and she had a hard time accepting the fact that she found him so darned attractive.

He walked to the far edge and dropped down, and she sat down next to him. She had accidentally—at least she thought it was accidentally—brushed her leg against his. He handed her the bottle of Ting. They remained quiet, wrapped only in the sound of the waves. His leg hairs tickled her as she swung her legs in rhythm with his.

"You don't like to talk much, do you?" she said when she couldn't stand the silence anymore.

"Silence is better. It's nice to absorb the atmosphere."

"But it's weird for two people to not talk to each other."

He tilted his head. "Why?"

"Well, I don't know why, it just is. When you're sitting with someone, you feel, I don't know, obligated to make conversation."

"I got out of that whole social obligation stuff a long time ago. In fact, some of my best relationships were with women who couldn't speak English. We sat in silence and enjoyed each other's company without having to talk about stuff."

She could easily picture him with some exotic beauty, sitting face-to-face, absorbing each other. She didn't want to picture it, though, and that worried her. She shouldn't care. "I don't imagine they last very long, those relationships."

"Nope."

"That doesn't seem to bother you terribly."

"Nope." He stared out over the water for a minute, looking at peace with himself. She noticed he'd set his beer to the side, untouched. "Ever been snorkeling or diving?"

"No way."

He took her hand and pulled her so that she was looking over the water. His touch startled her, so out of the blue, but she leaned forward next to him.

"Aren't you curious about what's down there?"

"I looked at the aquariums in the park."

He shook his head. "But seeing them in *their* world is completely different."

"There are lots of *things* down there." She tried to look beyond the reflection to what lurked beneath: rocks and coral, things that looked like fingers swirling in the water and two little black fish that were either courting or fighting. For some reason they reminded her of herself and Chris.

"And all those—" he glanced at her with a sideways smile "—*things* are happy in their world, just like you're happy in yours. Just because we can keep them doesn't mean we should. That's why I went to jail."

She blinked. "I think I missed something here."

"For most of the nine years I worked at Aquatic Wonders, I thought the dolphins were happy. Most people do, because we *want* to."

Her words echoed through her mind: *Very happy. Ecstatically happy.* She nodded, pushing the thought away. "Even Liberty looks happy. I mean, he has that smile."

"That's only a physical trait, an illusion much like an

alligator's so-called leering grin. Dolphins can be miserable and still look happy. Which is too bad. I wish they could look unhappy. Anyway, I grew up on a fishing charter boat. I'd seen dolphins ride the bow wake, but never swam with them. That's why the Aquatic Wonders job sounded so good. I thought I knew a lot about dolphins. I considered myself their ally and friend, and they trusted me.

"Then the park changed owners, and things went downhill for the dolphins. They cut back on the quality of the fish we fed them, cut back on the hours we worked with them and separated the dolphins instead of keeping them all together in their pen."

"But they're social creatures," she said, remembering Chris saying that before.

He took in her heartfelt words, and his gaze softened. The way she felt with him looking at her like that...he abruptly turned toward the ocean and continued. "I tried to tell the owner that, but he had several other small parks throughout the country, and this was the way they treated all their dolphins. I spent every spare minute, even my off time, with them so they wouldn't be lonely.

"One day I went diving off the coast and a pod of dolphins swam right past me. I watched them play and swim and interact, and I realized how different they were from the ones I worked with. They *felt* different. They were happy." He looked right into her eyes. "Really happy."

"Happy," she repeated softly, held spellbound by the passion in his eyes.

"Everything changed after that. I wanted to free the five dolphins we had in captivity. I talked to the manager, the new owner, everyone involved with the park, but no one wanted to listen. A newspaper reporter heard about the stink and interviewed me, and as soon as the article hit, I was fired.

"The thought of leaving those dolphins with no one to fight for them rattled me. So I went out to the pens that were situated on the water and cut the fence to free the dolphins. But they wouldn't go. I pushed, teased and even physically moved them out of the pens. The dolphins returned. That's when I learned that you couldn't just free them. How would they survive after eating dead fish for so long?

"The new owner had me arrested for vandalism, so I went public with the high mortality rate of the dolphins at marine parks, something that gets sympathy easily, if briefly. I spent a couple of days in jail before we came to terms—he wouldn't press charges, and he wouldn't release the dolphins. I got a few articles and TV coverage and that was it.

"But after that, I was deemed the fighter for dolphins. I started the Free Dolphin Society, got a few backers, and tried to fight Aquatic Wonders. I wanted the dolphins freed. They publicly agreed to some concessions, but I lost the big fight. I thought it was over, but it was only beginning. People started writing, calling, coming to my door to tell me about dolphin abuses. And like my friends at Aquatic Wonders, I couldn't turn my back on them either. So I continued my fight."

Her chest felt compressed, but he shrugged, as though it were all such a little deal.

"Don't look at me like that, Lucy," he said in a soft voice, using her name without the *Miz* for the first time. "It's just what I do."

"I know, I know, you're not a hero."

"Nope. I put some of those dolphins where they are."

"But if you hadn't, someone else would have."

He shook his head. "Doesn't matter. It was me."

She took a deep breath, confused by the swirl of feelings this man evoked inside her. He was an enigma, to be sure. And he believed in what he did in a way that was different than the way she believed in what she did. *You tout toilet paper, and he saves dolphins.*

Their gazes held again, and a charge arced between them. He leaned forward. She tilted her chin up. He looked at her mouth with a kind of hunger she knew was reflected in her eyes, too. She was captured in the green of his eyes, deeper than the depths of the sea and even more mysterious. The kiss took her by surprise, even though she wanted it with every cell of her body. It was a chaste kiss, yet it spoke of hot, steamy Caribbean nights and naked bodies beneath a full moon. His mouth covered her without hesitation, moving slowly back and forth, drawing out the kiss. Just as her body was on the verge of liquefying, she pulled back.

She gathered her thoughts as best as she could, but her voiced was slurred when she said, "You kissed me."

"And you kissed me back." He stood and held out his hand to her. His fingers felt strong as they wrapped around hers and lifted her to her feet. He pulled her up too fast, though, pitching her forward. She braced herself against his chest, and he grabbed her shoulders.

She said, "But you started it."

His mouth quirked in a smile. "Yeah, now that we got that out of the way, we can go back to disliking each other." He glanced up at the gray clouds that were now thin streaks across the sky. "Let's head back to the park. It looks like the lightning's over, and I've got a lot of work to do with Liberty."

Dislike him? After that kiss? "I guess I'll go back, too. I

need some time to think about Crandall's offer." And that kiss.

"You're not going to sell your place to that guy, are you?" he asked.

"Why not?"

"He looks slimy."

"You mean I'm supposed to tell him, 'You're slimy so I'm not going to deal with you'?"

"Yeah, why not?"

"Sorry, that's not my style."

"No, I suppose not. Of course not, what was I thinking?"

She paused, looking up at him. "You're picking on me again. I thought we'd come to a, well, sort of peace treaty. You did kiss me, after all. You must like me a little."

He ran his finger down her cheek. "You know as well as I do that two people who dislike each other don't kiss like that. And if we kiss that well, just think what else we could do...well. And thinking about that could be very distracting to a man like me who has a dolphin to see to. And to a woman like you who has a marine park to see to. For now, I think we should forget about that kiss and pretend it never happened."

Pretend it never happened? Oh, right. And with the way he was looking at her mouth, and slowly rubbing his own...like that was going to happen.

6

"Women are women are women," Chris said, tempting Liberty closer with a fish. Not all women left their bodily impressions on him for an hour after they'd been pressed together on the moped, and not all of them looked so cute, even dripping wet. Certainly not all of them felt as good under his mouth. "Women are women are women," he muttered again, and Liberty poked his head out of the water and nodded in agreement. For that, he got the fish.

"Ah, but you'd say anything for a fish. And you're smitten with her, too."

Chris had no objection to occasional female company, but Lucy wasn't going to be that company. She was a different breed, and he had no business even being distracted by the likes of her.

But he was.

And he didn't like it one bit.

So why had he kissed her earlier? She'd clearly wanted to know, but he didn't have an answer. He hadn't thought about it, considered the ramifications, or the wisdom of it. He'd simply kissed her, and he would have kissed her more if she hadn't backed up. In retrospect, he was glad she'd broken it off. At that moment, he hadn't been too happy about it.

Movement from the corner of his eye brought his gaze to her as she made her way over to Liberty's pool. Her dark hair had dried straight, curling under her chin and framing her face. He averted his gaze to the muscles in her legs as she walked, shapely, smooth legs—he looked back at Liberty.

"Hi," she said, tucking her hands into the pockets of her shorts.

He had to stop this.

"Hi," he said, though he barely glanced her way, barely enough to notice her nose was pinkening. He pulled another fish from the bucket and sank beneath the water. Liberty's form loomed before him; he was obviously intrigued by the human-beneath-the-water trick.

When Chris came up for air, he hoped she would be gone. She was seated by the edge of the pool instead. This bothered him, more so for the fact that the realization created a warm spot inside him. More so because he wanted to kiss her again. Since forming the Free Dolphin Society, he had become good at being rude or ignoring people who impeded his progress. He already knew Lucy couldn't be ignored, so he had to resort to the rude tactic.

He stopped what he was doing and looked at her with a tilt of his head, trying not to smile or look too deeply into those big brown eyes. "Don't you have some slimy real-estate guy to see?"

"Why, am I bothering you?"

"Yes." When she pulled her legs in defensively, he added, "It's nothing personal. Heck, you're better looking than the guys who work here."

She waved her hand coquettishly. "You charmer, you."

He held back a smile. "Hey, I never said I was good at dealing with people, did I? When I get to a place like this, I usually have to deal with an irate owner who bugs me until he realizes he can't make me budge, and then he leaves me alone."

"Ah, that's how you got so good at ignoring people."

"Exactly," he said with a smile. He was still smiling. "Besides, you're getting a nasty burn. You should put some sunblock on." Geez, so much for being rude. He sounded like her damned mother!

She cocked her head, giving him a wrinkle-nosed smile. "Thanks for caring."

He focused on Liberty again. "Don't mention it."

"I'll try to hold myself back," she said.

A thin voice floated over the wind from the front gate. "Yoo-hoo, Lucy!" Crandall stood at the gate with the closed sign hanging on the other side.

She waved him in. "It's not locked."

The guy looked impeccable, even in the humid, heavy air. And he was as slick and slimy as the fish Chris held in his hand.

"So, Mr. Slick's back to work some moves on you again, eh?" he said as the man approached with his hundred-watt smile in place.

She shot Chris a look that might have melted a lesser man. "I can take care of myself." She turned to give Crandall a much nicer smile, standing to take his outstretched hand. "Hello, Mr. Sl—Morton." She shot Chris another irritated look, but he could only grin at her faux pas.

Crandall held her hand for far longer than a normal handshake. "I'm sorry we haven't been able to give you nicer weather today," he said, glancing up at the streaky, gray sky.

"And you would be the weather god, then?" Chris asked, unable to resist.

Crandall aimed the smile at him. "Of course not. Just

a—" back to Lucy "—spokesman for our island." Then back to Chris. "I don't believe we've met."

"That's because we haven't."

She rolled her eyes. "This is Chris Maddox—"

Crandall nodded. "The dolphin thief, I presume." He smiled at her as though the three of them were in on some joke together.

Chris was about to explain the misunderstanding, but she beat him to it. "Chris has legal custody of Liberty. Now, I'm afraid I haven't given much thought to your earlier offer. I've been—" he swore he saw a slight flush rise up her already pink face "—enjoying the scenery."

"Actually, I stopped by to see if you had changed your mind about joining me for dinner tonight."

Brother, he *was* going to put the moves on her. Chris felt himself wanting to intercede on her behalf, to say they already had plans. But he wasn't a hero and he wasn't interested in Lucy, so he turned back to Liberty. Besides, didn't she just tell him she could take care of herself? He didn't miss the glance she slid his way before saying, "I'd be glad to. After all, I don't have any other plans."

"Wonderful," Crandall said, sliding her arm into the crook of his own and leading her away from the pool like she was some princess. Well, she was the advertising princess, wasn't she?

"I was thinking white wine, lobster and watching what might be a spectacular sunset later on if it clears."

She looked at Chris, and that strange heroic impulse to call her back rose in his throat. He swallowed it down and turned away. She turned back, too, laughing overly loud at something Mr. Slick said.

"Women are women are women," he said, giving Liberty the last fish in the bucket. He walked over to the edge of the pool and grabbed the raft. This was what he wanted. So why did he feel disappointed?

LUCY FELT a little stab of disappointment when Chris turned away from her. What did she expect?

Crandall had her arm tightly tucked in his, going on about the weather patterns in the Bahamas. She pulled away as soon as they neared the entrance in preparation to open the gate, which could actually be done one-handed. Once it was relatched, she kept her arm a safe distance from Crandall.

Wait a minute. What was wrong with her? She'd cuddled up to Chris on a very small seat earlier—and enjoyed it, if she had to be honest with herself—yet this respectable man who at least wore *clothes* merely wanted to hold her hand, and she felt hesitant. If this man kissed her, he probably wouldn't then turn around and say they should forget it.

He opened the car door for her as he told her about the charming restaurant he was part owner of that he was taking her to. She didn't even realize at first that the car was backward, with the driver's side on the right. She slid into the import that was clean and new, but found her gaze on the old moped leaning against the side gate.

"Should I change into something nicer?" she asked, wrenching her attention from the moped. "I'm a bit wrinkled."

"No, you look charming. Besides, we're very casual down here. You'll fit right in."

He drove as crazily as the natives, but apologized every time she reached for the strap. He spent the drive to the restaurant talking about himself, a subject he seemed quite enamored of.

She thought of the differences between Chris and

Crandall, focusing on the latter's positive traits. "You know, it's refreshing to hear a man talk about himself after being with Chris, who only talks about himself under duress."

"I've heard about him. He's some kind of dolphin freedom fighter, isn't he?"

She smiled. "Dolphin freedom fighter. I like that."

He waved off the subject with a flip of his hand. They pulled beneath a portico, and two young men ran out and opened their doors, bowing as though Crandall was royalty. Well, he certainly acted that way, holding his thin frame erect, patrician nose in the air. Her mother would approve, to be sure.

The host led them to a table by the windows that lined the entire back of the restaurant. After approving the wine, Crandall ordered for them, and they were left alone. The sunset was not spectacular, and the dark green water stretched restlessly out until it kissed the sky. She took a deep, quiet breath and drank it in. It wasn't pretty, but it was peaceful. For the first time, she wanted to sit there and absorb.

With a smile, she turned to Crandall as his mouth opened to say something. "Can we just...you know, sit here for a minute without saying anything?"

He looked at her as though she'd asked for a hot dog and fries. "Why would you want to do that?"

Her smile widened, because hadn't she said the same thing to Chris? "To absorb." The way Chris had explained it made sense, but she couldn't remember his exact words. "Never mind."

He gathered her hands in his across the small tabletop. "Good, because I want to talk to you, Lucy. First, a little business to get out of the way, and then we can...absorb each other's company." He gave her a patronizing smile along with a squeeze of her hands. "The investors are anxious to hear about their offer on your property."

"I told you, I haven't decided yet. If they're in that big of a hurry, let them buy something else."

He nodded. "I told them you were not a lady to be rushed."

"You did, did you?"

"Certainly." The man had poise, she had to give him that.

"Good, because it's true. Besides, I kind of like owning a bit of property in the Bahamas, and I want to enjoy it."

"Business over then," he said, tipping his wineglass against hers.

She took a sip of her wine. "You know, it is so refreshing to talk to someone...civilized. I think Chris is part dolphin, and he has no manners, no chivalry. I fell into the dolphin's pool my first day here, and you know what he does? He dries himself off with a towel and then hands it to me to use." She found herself laughing at the memory. "Oh, he did help me out of the pool, I'll give him credit for that." With his hands on her behind, his strong fingers molding her curves....

The waiter brought plates of broiled lobster, and she found herself glad she didn't opt for silence. She was having fun talking.

"And so he got arrested for trying to free these dolphins. Can you believe someone would have such conviction to risk going to jail? I can't think of one thing I believe in that strongly. Can you? But when I watch him work with Liberty, I see why he feels so strongly about them.

"Aw, you should have seen Liberty toss that ball to me. You would have fallen right in love with him. And I fed him a fish! Well, not the first time when Chris threw one in my lap. But I actually handed Liberty a fish, and he took it from me!" She clasped her hands together, shaking her head. "It was amazing! Chris thinks they're smarter than people. He certainly thinks they're better than people."

He was looking very relaxed after his fifth glass of wine. Every time she took a sip, he'd fill her glass again.

"I'm fine," she said after the eighth time he'd done this.

"But you're not drinking, you're too busy talking."

"I'm not much of a drinker."

When the waiter took their plates away, he tossed his linen napkin on the table. "You don't want dessert, do you?"

"I shouldn't. But thank you for...asking." His charm was wearing thin, or perhaps it was his patience, though she couldn't imagine why. "Thank you very much for a lovely dinner."

His smile quickly resumed. "You're very welcome, my dear. Please allow me to take you around our little island and show you some of the sights."

"Well, I really should be getting back—"

He cut her off by squeezing her hand. "Please, I want to show you a few of the special places on the island. Then I promise I'll leave you alone and let you make your decision about the property."

She hesitated, but figured she could go along since he'd treated her to this wonderful dinner. "All right, perhaps for a short while."

CHRIS PULLED HIMSELF from the pool and dried off. His enthusiasm over Liberty's acceptance had waned somewhat while he'd sprawled out on the raft and thought of nothing in particular. Especially not Lucy having dinner with Mr. Slick. He shrugged into a shirt and stepped into a pair of shorts. His big plans for the night included going over the dolphin's medical history and preparing a chart to track his progress.

"Hey, dolphin mon!"

Chris looked up to find Bailey walking over with something less than a hostile expression on his face. "What's up?"

"Do you know where Miss Lucy be? She usually be hanging around wit' you, mon."

Chris rubbed the back of his neck. "Well, I don't think she'll be doing that anymore. She's having dinner with Mr. Slick of the real estate company."

Bailey's eyes widened, making him look comical. "Oh, no, he's probably taking her to his fancy restaurant, da Blue Conch, giving her da whole dine and wine t'ing. You let her leave wit' dat man?"

"She didn't exactly ask my permission." But he couldn't help remember the look on her face as she'd glanced back at him before they'd left. "Why, what's wrong with her having dinner with the guy, except that he's probably a jerk." Something cold settled into his bones. "That is all he is, isn't it?"

Bailey flattened his palm on his forehead. "I don' know, mon. Morton be a bad mon eenai' place, you know what I mean?"

"No, explain it to me."

"He jus' gonna charm her right into signing dose papers. He got ways of charming a woman."

Chris relaxed again. "Is that all? I mean, she's not in danger, is she?"

"Jus' maybe her virtue. And her common sense. Dat man can be pushy, if you know what I mean."

"Maybe you didn't notice, but Miz Lucy's a smart

lady. She's not going to let any two-bit mambo talk her into anything she doesn't want. She can take care of herself, believe me."

Bailey didn't look convinced. "I've got a friend who might be interested in dis place. I don't want her to make any fast decisions without getting to talk to her."

"Miz Lucy's not the impulsive type." Then he remembered their ride on the moped. "Most of the time. You can talk to her in the morning."

"Okay, mon."

Chris followed Bailey out, glancing up as the lights over the park came on with a crackling noise. Bailey got into his little car and sped away, but Chris sat on the moped and wondered why his paperwork wasn't calling so loudly anymore.

CRANDALL'S MOOD lifted once they left the restaurant. He drove slowly through the town and pointed out different structures he had a hand in selling. She'd noticed the bottle of wine and two glasses he'd taken from the Blue Conch, but wasn't in the mood for any more wine. Or any more Crandall, actually.

"This has all been fascinating," she said, stifling a yawn, "but I'm beat. You can drop me off at the park if you don't mind." She didn't want Crandall to know where she was staying.

"But I've got wine."

"I don't want any more wine. Like I said, I'm beat."

"One more stop, and I'll take you back. You'll love this place."

She let out a soft sigh. "All right, one more stop."

A short while later he pulled down a white driveway that disappeared into lush foliage. A beautiful house sat at the end of a driveway lit with large bulbs atop black posts.

"Crandall, what is this?"

"My place."

"I'm not going inside." Impatience turned to uneasiness. Wasn't he just like the men she dated up north, she thought. Trying to impress her with what they had, thinking that would be the aphrodisiac to lull her into bed.

"No, it's not like that," he said, taking her hand and placing it against his lips. He opened the door and got out, then held her door open. "I want to show you the beach. You can't see it from here, but it's just behind the house. I own a stretch of private beach here, the most beautiful beach in the world."

"Wouldn't it be better to see it during the day?"

"It's more beautiful at night."

She reluctantly got out of the car, glancing skyward to find it still obliterated in clouds. Once in a while slivers of the moon would peek out, but other than that it was dark. He took her arm and led her down a stone pathway to the beach. She could hear the waves washing in, but the ocean was a vast, dark pit beyond the ornamental lights on the back lawn.

Despite her earlier statement, he poured a glass of wine and handed it to her, then poured his own and made an indent in the sand with the bottle. While he was doing that, she poured out some of her wine. She hovered near the light, but he took her arm and pulled her down the wide beach that faded to noisy blackness.

"You think I brought you here to seduce you, Lucy? To charm you into accepting my investors' offer?"

"Perhaps," she said, trying to tactfully free herself

from him. "Shall I save you time and tell you now that it won't work?"

They had reached the outer limit of the light. He abruptly stopped and turned her to face him.

"Did it occur to you that you are an attractive woman, and I am an attractive man, and that I want to get to know you better? On a personal level."

She would have laughed at his statement if she weren't so nervous. "Well, I, uh, appreciate that." She cleared her throat of the lie. "But I'm not looking for that right now."

He moved closer. "I wasn't so sure about that, with the way you kept talking about the guy with the dolphin, all night talk, talk, talk."

She shrank away at his harsh tone. "I find him fascinating. The dolphin, I mean."

His annoyance evaporated. "Mmm. I find you fascinating." He pulled her closer. "We could have a good time together while you're down here, deal or not. Would you like that?"

She could feel the hardness of him pushing against her stomach, which was lurching crazily. She pushed him away. "No, I wouldn't. I want to go home now." She started walking toward the car, but he grabbed her arm and pulled her back.

"Now, Lucy, don't walk off in a huff." His fingers stroked down her cheek. "Every woman wants a tropical fling. I can make your fantasies come to life. You could stay here for the rest of your visit instead of that cracker box your father lived in."

She stiffened and tried to move away, but he held her fast. "How did you know where I was staying?"

He smiled, as though he'd paid her some great compliment by snooping into her life. She could see the wine-tinged haze in his eyes. "I did some checking. Stop being so defensive. I'm not some maniac. Most women would consider themselves lucky to have a man like me ready to take them to paradise. Come on, Lucy. Give in to your desires." His grip tightened on her wrists. "You know you want me."

Her whole body was trembling, but it wasn't with desire. Everything was quiet, deadly quiet. His own personal paradise, he'd said. Her own private hell. Well, she wasn't going to give him anything without a heck of a fight. She closed her eyes and readied her knee to come up between his legs.

7

BEFORE LUCY COULD get her knee up, Crandall twisted her into an embrace that rendered that move impossible. His lips sealed over hers as his hands held hers in a tight grip. This could not be happening. This had to be a misunderstanding or a nightmare. She tried shaking her head to free herself of his kiss.

And then she heard the whistling.

He looked shocked that anyone would dare intrude on his private beach, but hot relief washed over her when she looked over and saw the silhouette of a man walking in the outer fringe of darkness, whistling a jaunty tune. Whistling "Margaritaville." She stumbled away from Crandall, but he snagged her wrist before she could get far.

"Honey, be careful. You never know what kind of bum is going to come down that beach, even though it is fenced in on either side."

She watched the form walk closer, her stomach in knots. A savior or some drunk? She held her breath, waiting. Then her face broke into a huge smile when Chris walked into the light. But how would he even be on this side of the island? It didn't matter, it was him. Her body went to jelly, but she summoned her courage. No way was that man leaving without her.

Chris was looking ahead, but glanced their way with a surprised expression on his face. "Oh, excuse me. Didn't mean to disturb you." He continued walking forward, but his pace slowed.

Crandall's grip tightened on her wrist. "This is a private beach. If you don't vacate the premises immediately, I'll call the police."

Chris stopped and turned toward them, making a shelf over his eyes with his hand. "Morton, is that you?" He walked toward them, and then seemed surprised to see her. "Lucy! Fancy meeting you here." He held out a hand to Crandall, which necessitated his letting go of her hand to shake it. She stumbled away.

"I, uh, what are you doing here?" Crandall said, now clenching his hands at his sides.

Chris nodded toward the beach behind him. "Just taking a walk. Did you know this is supposed to be the most beautiful beach in the world?" He looked at her, and she saw a gleam in his eyes. So, he'd been listening to them all along. She found herself wanting to run to his arms, but held herself back.

Crandall stiffened. "Yes, and it's a private beach. If you don't mind, Lucy and I were getting to know each other."

Just before Crandall's arm slid around her shoulders, Chris took a step forward and pulled her close to his side.

"But, Lucy, you promised me a beer later at Barney's, remember?"

"I, uh, yes!" She tapped her forehead with the heel of her shaking hand. "How could I forget?" She looked at Crandall, hoping the strain in her voice wasn't obvious. "I owe him a beer." Chris's lean, hard body was pressed up against hers. She pressed even closer.

Crandall gave Lucy a stern look. "You said you didn't have any plans tonight."

"I forgot about the beer."

"For saving her life earlier," Chris said with a nod.

"She fell into the stingray pit, and I pulled her out in the nick of time."

"I thought you fell into the dolphin's pool," Crandall said.

She nodded vigorously, giving him an overly bright smile. "That, too. Guess I'm pretty clumsy."

Chris winked. "Got to keep a close eye on this one. Are you ready for that beer now, or do you want me to come back and get you later?"

"Might as well go now." She turned to Crandall, feeling anger now replace her fear. "Thank you for dinner. The food was great. And the company," she gave him her sweetest smile, "I could feed to the sharks without remorse."

Chris shrugged, turning her toward the house. "Women. They're moodier than the weather." She was still tucked in the crook of his arm as they made their way to the driveway where his moped was parked in the shadows.

Crandall followed them, watching with a suspicious expression. Chris straddled the bike and she slid up behind him, putting her arms around him and pressing her cheek against his back. He started the bike, waved at Crandall and sped away.

She let out a long, guttural scream as they sped through the night. "Oh *gawd*, I can't believe him! He was disgusting. His lips touched mine!" She rubbed her lips back and forth against his shirt, wanting to rub off at least two layers of skin. Her body starting trembling as she realized what might have happened.

"You all right?" he called out over the wind.

She shook her head, rocking her cheek back and forth against him when he stopped at an intersection. "You saved my life!"

"Nah. Maybe your virtue."

"Careful...your chivalry is showing."

He glanced back at her with a grin. "Oh, how embarrassing."

A few minutes later they pulled into Barney's crowded parking lot. Before he turned the engine off, he twisted around. "Are you ready for that beer?"

She looked at the lights and the people inside, happy music filling the air. "I'm not really in the mood to be around a bunch of people."

"Want me to take you to your father's apartment?"

She shook her head. "He knows where I'm staying."

He nodded, and then headed north again. She closed her eyes and tried to push away images of Crandall. It was all she could do to hold on, to fight the trembling and weakness that filled her. The could-have-beens pounded through her the way the wind rushed past her ears.

Then the wind lessened, and the road turned into crunching white gravel. She opened her eyes to find they'd turned onto a driveway not unlike Crandall's. But this time a wood sign announced The Caribe Plantation. The drive wound past a mansion that looked stately and pristine, columns towering along the front porch. Huge pots of ferns were spaced evenly between the columns. Surrounding the mansion, and flanking it from both the road and the beach was a beautiful garden.

He parked the bike and helped her off, then led her down a wooden boardwalk that stretched over the water to structure of some sort. A boat was parked beneath a covered dock on one side, but they walked around to the other side where a deck and two lounge chairs awaited them. He walked inside a door and turned on a light that washed the deck with its warmth. She dropped to the edge of one of the chairs and wrapped her arms around herself, staring out into the dark ocean. Shivers washed over her in synch with the sound of the ocean washing onto the shore nearby.

He emerged and handed her an icy bottle of Ting, then sat down across from her. "Unless you'd like something stronger?"

"No, this is fine, thank you." She noticed he'd taken a soda for himself, too. Their knees nearly touched, and she could feel the hairs on his legs tickling her skin. She pulled her gaze to his.

"Thank you for what you did," she said softly.

"No problem, mon."

"Don't make light of it. You really could have saved my life, you know."

"You could have handled it, Miz Lucy. But I think he was anticipating the knee thing, and I wasn't sure you could get him from that angle."

"You were so...subtle about it all." She found herself smiling. "And that whistling."

He took a sip of his soda and set it down on the floor. "I wasn't sure if you were just playing coy with him, so I figured I'd show up and give you an out. When I saw the look on your face, I knew you weren't comfortable."

She shook her head. "That's an understatement. But you were listening to us the whole time, weren't you?" She smiled again, imitating him. "'Did you know this is supposed to be the most beautiful beach in the world?'" This time her laughter chased away the trembling. "That was great! And the stingray thing. Where did you come up with that stuff?"

"Ah, I was making it up as I went along."

Her smile faded. "But how did you know? You didn't just happen to be on that beach, did you?"

He glanced away, obviously uncomfortable with being heroic. Something inside her warmed at that thought.

"Bailey was concerned about you going to dinner with the guy. He didn't think Crandall was dangerous, just pushy. I told him you could take care of yourself, and I believed that. But I found myself going toward the Blue Conch."

Her eyes widened "You followed us from there?"

"All over this piece of paradise."

She chewed her bottom lip, trying not to let out the smile that would probably scare him away. "Thank you."

"You already thanked me."

"I can't thank you enough." She looked down at the already sweating bottle clasped in her hands. "I was scared, Chris. I was trying not to be, but I was."

He reached over and tilted up her chin. "You're welcome."

When she met his gaze, her stomach dropped right out of her. She sucked in a quick breath and looked away.

"I'm only glad you weren't falling for that guy's charm," he said, standing and leaning against the railing.

"And what charm was that?" She stood too, leaning her back against the railing. "He's not my type."

"Now, Miz Lucy, I thought that was exactly the kind of guy you'd go for."

The way he said her name shimmered right down her back. She glanced sideways and found him turned toward her, a teasing grin on his face.

"Okay, I'll admit that's the type of guy I usually go for. But not him specifically, and not that 'give in to your desires' stuff. He had to show me everything he'd sold, tell me everything he's done. It was pitiful."

"When there's nothing inside, people have to compensate by having a lot of stuff on the outside."

She tilted her head. "So you think because I have a Beemer and a diamond watch that I don't have anything on the inside?"

He leaned closer. "I'm not talking about you. I'm talking about people who flaunt it."

"Oh."

He stayed there for a moment, close enough that if she leaned forward just a bit they'd be kissing. In that suspended moment, she felt alive.

"Lucy?" he said softly.

"Mmm?"

"Don't keep looking at me like that, or I'll have to kiss you again, and neither one of us really wants that, do we?"

She blinked, breaking out of the spell she'd been held in. Her heart was thudding like crazy. "No, of course not."

"No." He straightened, taking another swig of Ting as though it was a beer. "You're welcome to stay here tonight if you want. It's not much, a bunkhouse—"

"That would be great. Seriously," she added at his questioning look.

"I was going to say that there's only one room in there."

"Fine."

"And an outdoor shower."

"I don't care." When he continued to look at her as though he couldn't believe what she was saying, she added, "Listen, I've had a rough night. I could have you take me to some hotel, but I don't want to put you out any more than I already have." Her voice softened. "And

I don't want to be alone tonight." She cleared her throat. "But I do need to wash up."

He nodded, but his gaze held hers for a moment. "Shower's around the corner." She followed him to the side of the building that faced the dark ocean and found the showerhead he was pointing at.

"Boy, you weren't kidding about the outdoor shower."

"Nope, I'd never kid about anything like that with a woman like you." He ignored her questioning look. "I've never seen anyone out there. If you don't mind washing up in near darkness, you should feel pretty private back here. Want to go first?"

"Sure."

"I'll get you a shirt, but I don't think you're going to fit into my shorts."

"I'll wear these, but the shirt'll be great." She glanced down and then back up at him. "Thanks, Chris."

"No problem. Shampoo and soap are right there, and I'll bring you a washcloth and towel."

He returned with the items he promised and left her to shower in the absolute open. Over the sound of the water, Jimmy Buffett sang, "Changes in Latitudes, Changes in Attitudes." Lord, would she ever have thought she'd be doing this?

"Okay, let's get this over with," she muttered, stripping out of her clothes and stepping beneath the cool water. She reached for the heat adjustment and found none. Standing naked in front of miles of open ocean made her feel even more naked, if that was possible. But it also made her feel sensual, adventurous. As the washcloth slid over her body, she couldn't help but wonder how Chris's hands would feel doing the same thing. Or better yet, how his mouth...

Stop!

She quickly finished, then slipped into a well-worn but clean cotton shirt that hung halfway to her knees.

When she rounded the corner, he gave her a sheepish smile. "I forgot to tell you there wasn't warm water, didn't I?"

"Yes, but I figured it out very quickly."

"And you still didn't change your mind about the hotel?"

"Maybe I'm tougher than you think I am," she said as they passed each other on the deck. Or maybe she was just lonelier, she added.

She felt cool and refreshed, looking out over the vast blackness of the ocean, listening to the water splashing over his body and the waves splashing against the pilings below. This was his life, she thought, closing her eyes and trying to imagine what it was like. Living like this, in boathouses with no warm water or private shower, no turndown service. No having a regular job to get up and get ready for every morning. They were two different people brought together by a dolphin.

"You look very relaxed for a woman whose virtue was threatened less than an hour ago," he said from behind her a few minutes later.

"Mmm, I'm trying to forget about that."

He wore a pair of cut-offs and absolutely nothing else except for the necklace and bracelet. She felt a hitch in her chest and cleared her throat. He picked up his bottle and settled back on the lounge chair. She sat down across from him, finding herself leaning forward and stroking the rough edges of his necklace.

"Is it a shark's tooth?" She was staring at it, and when she looked up at him, she realized they were too close for comfort. With a quick breath, she moved away.

He watched her, his eyes analytical. "Yep."

"Why do you wear such a thing?"

"When I was sixteen, this was imbedded in my arm." He twisted his arm, and she could see a faint scar running from shoulder midway to his elbow.

"Ouch. And you *wear* it?"

"A reminder that I'm not invincible."

She leaned on her arm, propping up her chin with the palm of her hand. "And the bracelet?"

"A college student I met a few years ago made it for me. She was into that kind of thing, making bracelets with these colored threads."

She felt a strange twist in her stomach. She pictured a young, lithe blonde hanging on his shoulder. "And this reminds you of her?"

"No, it reminds me not to get attached to anything or anyone. She was working on a marine biology project, so I let her hang around for a few months. Kid thought she was in love with me, wanted to give up everything and follow me around the world." His smile was both wistful and cynical. "I knew she'd outgrow it, and she did."

"So you got attached to her?"

"I liked having her around." He looped his finger around the band. "This reminds me to keep my head straight."

"Ah, I see." So, someone had gotten to him, at least in a marginal way. Maybe he was human after all. "No wife?"

He laced his fingers behind his head, distracting her for a moment with his biceps.

"This may surprise you, but traveling all over and dealing with fish doesn't have a big appeal to most women. I get my company when I can take it."

She remembered the women he'd told her about who sat there and said nothing with him. But she didn't want silence now, not when he was actually talking to her. She took another sip of her Ting, which was already warm.

"You said you grew up on a fishing charter boat."

"After my mother died when I was just a kid, my father sunk all our money into a fishing boat down in the Keys that we also lived on. He usually had two fishing charters a day, one scheduled for right after I got back from school. If I didn't come right home, he'd fillet me just like the fish I helped the customers catch and clean."

"Your dad abused you?" She felt angry at the thought, all tight inside.

"I wouldn't call it abuse. He was oppressive. He worked me hard and he yelled a lot. Geez, Lucy, don't look so mad. I was a tough kid. I survived."

She glanced away for a moment, taking the pained expression from her face. "I'm sorry."

"Don't be. It wasn't all bad. I spent every spare moment I had in the water. I traded some fish for a friend's mask when I was ten, then saved every penny I could get my hands on to buy a snorkel. The world beneath the water was magical, mysterious, endless. I wanted to explore every inch of it. In that quiet world, I couldn't hear my father yelling. There was only the ocean and the thousands of creatures within it.

"When I was thirteen, I lied about my age and got certified to scuba dive. Diving made me feel a real part of that underwater life for the first time. Like the fish, I didn't have to go up for air."

"What happened after that?"

He met her gaze, making her realize how anxious she sounded. "Why do you want to know?"

"I just do." She used the same tactic he'd used on her, waiting patiently for him to continue.

"I left home when I was sixteen, tired of having to deal

with my father, tired of life at sea. But being alone, being a loner, had been ingrained into my soul, and that I remained. I knew I wouldn't leave the water far behind as I made my way up the Keys. I had no use for any other kind of life.

"Then I found the job at Aquatic Wonders. They needed someone to feed the dolphins, maintain the facility and be a general boy Friday. The thought of working with dolphins piqued my interest, and I took the job. So now you know more about me than probably anyone else."

Lucy couldn't help smiling. "Sometimes persistence pays."

He tipped his head back, looking up at the sky. "Beautiful and curious, just what I wanted."

Those words swirled through her stomach, but she couldn't think of any suitable reply.

"When do you go back home, Miz Lucy?"

"A couple of days from now." She was watching him carefully now. "Still eager to get rid of me?"

"Doesn't matter what I want. If you'll recall, I wanted you to leave me alone, and now you're sleeping over."

A warm flush crept up her cheeks. "Yeah, well." She met his gaze, but found only a relaxed expression on his face. "Do you still want me to leave you alone?"

"In a few days you'll go back to your life and your Beemer and your ex-husband and your business. I'll eventually free Liberty, go home for a while, then head off to another park and another dolphin."

Maybe that was his way of telling her that he didn't want her to leave him alone anymore. He was right: she was leaving soon, and they'd never see each other again. Her throat went dry at the thought, and she took another sip of Ting.

"Right now it's hard to believe I could be home in my apartment and not even know that anything like this place exists." Or anyone like him.

"This is only one of many, many places like this. I'll bet you're too busy to take vacations."

"Mostly."

"See, that's my problem with your kind of life. You work hard so you can afford nice things, and then you want nicer things, so you work harder, and pretty soon you work so much you don't have time to enjoy the nice things you're paying for."

"Maybe some of us don't like being a martyr."

He laughed. "You think that's what I am? A martyr?"

"Not exactly."

"It's hard for you to comprehend that someone doesn't want success, isn't it?"

She chewed her lip again. "Well, yes."

"Different worlds, you and I," he said, coming to his feet. "Come on, Miz Lucy. Let me show you to your hammock."

She followed him into the boathouse. "Er, did you say...hammock?"

8

LUCY STRETCHED in the early-morning light, reveling in the smile that made her feel alive and ready to conquer the world.

Smile?

She ran her finger over the curve of her lips. She *was* smiling. How long had it been since she'd woken up with a smile? The memory eluded her. A thousand birds chirped and sang outside, and sunshine filled the wooden interior of the boathouse. Even the large, padded hammock had been comfortable.

A bank of storage cabinets ran along one wall to a door that she hoped would reveal a bathroom. Two duffel bags and a wooden crate sat beneath a glassless window that looked back on the house. Next to the bags a guitar leaned against the wall. Chris's?

She scrambled out of the hammock and walked out onto the deck. A pillow and rumpled sheet covered the lounge chair where he had slept. She spotted him near the beach where some fishing nets made a half-moon in the water. He looked like some exotic island boy with his wild, golden curls and bare chest gleaming wet in the early sunshine. She passed off the twist in her stomach as a need to go, and went back inside.

As she made her way along the deck a few minutes later, she watched small schools of silvery fish moving in perfect unison against the backdrop of smooth, white sand. He crouched by the shore wearing headphones and turning the dial on some electronic box.

"Hi," she said, then touched his arm when he didn't hear her.

He smiled and took off the headphones. "Morning, sleepyhead."

She inhaled quickly to dispel the tightness his smile caused inside her. "When I wake up to this, I think I could live like this." *Look at the water, Lucy. That's what you're talking about. Isn't it?*

He followed her gaze oceanward. "As long as you know you've got a job and apartment back home."

"I suppose that's true." It was hard to believe she did have a home somewhere faraway. It was harder to believe she felt that way after only being away for four days.

"You know it's true." When she looked at him, his expression wasn't cynical. "I'm not saying it's a bad thing."

"Ahem. The Great Green Lie. Greedy, materialistic...ring any bells?"

He grinned again, and she tried to remember what they were talking about.

"Ah, you're not so bad, Miz Lucy."

She shivered, blaming it on the warm breeze. "Well, I guess that's a compliment."

"Closest you'll get from me. I'm long out of flattering practice."

She kicked at a wave that rolled in to tickle her toes. "Well, I got beautiful and curious out of you." She glanced at him. "I'd say I'm doing pretty good then."

He looked at her. "You're doing just fine."

The smile he gave her was slighter than the previous one, but it had no less of an effect on her heart. She averted her attention to the device sitting on the ground with the black cable snaking into the water.

"What is that?"

"It's a recorder. I'm making a tape of the sounds in this lagoon. I'm going to play them for Liberty so he'll get used to this place before I move him here." He looked out over the water. "From here, it's freedom."

"What kinds of sounds are out there, anyway? I mean, I always thought it was silent down there."

He placed the headphones over her ears. Their fingers touched when she pressed the earpieces closer. Why just that simple brush could send a thrill of excitement through her was a mystery. Her ex had to do a lot more than that to elicit that much of a thrill. She refocused on listening. There were sounds down there! Clicks, water rushing up on the shore, a low-pitched humming noise...a virtual cacophony.

She handed back the phones. "That is so neat. You're right, there is a whole different world down there."

He turned off the recorder and pulled in the rubber microphone. "I've got to swim out and check my traps tomorrow. What I get will be used as fish-catching training. Wanna come?"

His invitation took her off guard. Her usual routine was to get all details before committing to anything, which was why she was so surprised when her mouth said, "Sure." She glanced out to the ocean. "Out there, you mean?"

"That's where the fish are."

"In that boat?"

He started heading toward the boathouse. "Nope. We're going to swim out to them. With fins, mask, snorkel, that kind of thing. Then you can see what's making those noises."

She nodded, scrambling for an excuse to back out. Seasickness? Lame leg? Nah. Besides, he might not think she was all right anymore. Darn, what did it even matter?

"But I don't have any of that fin stuff you mentioned."

"There's some in the shed at the park. I saw it when I was looking for the pump equipment."

"Oh. Great."

When they got back to the boathouse, she gathered up her shirt and put on her shoes. "I guess I'll get a hotel room for my last two nights here." She glanced around, wondering where she could stay to get this kind of view in the morning. "I'd like to take some pictures."

He pulled on a T-shirt and baggy shorts. "Bring your camera when we go snorkeling tomorrow."

Snorkeling. The thought seized her with both panic and excitement. She was going to do it. No excuses. Wait till she told Vicki! Somehow she had to get a picture of Chris and Liberty, just to remember.

Like she'd ever forget.

LUCY SNUGGLED against Chris's back as he started the moped and headed toward town. There was something to be said for meager transportation.

Wait a minute. What was going on here? She wasn't supposed to be enjoying the warm feel of him against her cheek. Certainly not supposed to be relishing every dip in the road when her breasts slid across his back. Yes, it had been a while since she'd partaken in the sensual pleasures of life, but Chris wasn't her type. And flings...out of the question.

When they arrived at the park, she said, "Can you please give me a ride to my father's apartment later? I'll get a cab to the hotel from there."

He pushed the sunglasses he'd been wearing up a few

inches. "Miz Lucy, I'll take you anywhere you want to go on that moped." And then he walked off, just like that, to leave her wondering what he'd meant.

Bailey waved as he tossed chunks of fish into one of the pools. The chunks landed with a dull splash and quickly sank to the bottom where a disinterested shark hovered above the floor. The sign identified the brown creature with the round head as a nurse shark.

Bailey grinned widely, giving her a raised eyebrow and nod toward Chris. "Good morning, Miss Lucy." He looked at Chris. "Mister dolphin fish man. Miss Lucy, I need to talk to you today."

"Stop by when I'm in the office."

"Sure t'ing." He dropped one last piece of fish in the pool and wandered to the stingray pit.

"He's going to tell you about a friend who wants to buy this place."

"Well, I'm open for offers."

"Is that a fact?"

This time he met her questioning gaze, and it was Lucy who turned away. He was going to drive her crazy, to be sure. He squatted down to get a closer look at the shark. It was in a pool much smaller than Liberty's. She thought the shark looked bored and lonely.

"Is it dangerous? Like the kind you see in the movies?" She glanced at his necklace. "The kind that bit your arm?"

He trailed a finger along the surface of the water. "Nah, not this one. They're rather docile unless they're molested, which is why they're responsible for most shark bites. People tend to think they're tame, but they're still a wild creature. If you'd fallen into this pool, for instance, the shark would probably stay as far away from you as he could. If you grabbed him, though, he'd probably bite you." He stood and pulled his T-shirt off in one movement, revealing lean muscles and a taut stomach. "Off to work."

Liberty's head was already out of the water, as though he somehow sensed his hero had arrived.

"Lucy."

That particular voice crawled up her spine like the thought of touching dead fish. Worse than that! Crandall made his way over to her, an apologetic expression on his face. Of all the nerve. He seemed to sense her hostility and paused, his hands in midair.

"I have nothing to say to you, Mr. Morton. Please leave."

Out of the corner of her eye she could see Chris watching them. Even Liberty was observing. This time she didn't need anyone to come to her rescue.

Crandall tilted his head. "Lucy, I know I made a bad impression, and I apologize. I was getting signals—"

"You were *not* getting signals from me, buster."

He raised his hands. "I misinterpreted." His smile marked the skill of a true actor. "It was probably the wine. After you left, I felt...well, bad. I drove by your father's apartment, but you weren't there."

She was glad she'd been with Chris. Well, for more than that reason. "Fine, you've apologized. Now leave."

Crandall laughed softly. "Lucy, let's talk about this. I think we can come to an understanding."

She glanced down into the nurse shark's pool. "Are you familiar with sharks, Mr. Morton?"

He followed her gaze, taking the opportunity to step up beside her. "Not really."

She narrowed her eyes. "I'm surprised." Then she turned back to the shark. "This is one of the fiercest sharks known to man. Just a tad nicer than the great white shark. See those pieces of fish down there?" Crandall nodded, giving her a patronizing smile that would have grated on her nerves if she didn't already despise the man. "That was a whole fish when it went into the pool only moments ago." She tried not to grin at his widened eyes.

"Should we be inside the fence like this?"

"His teeth are this long." She indicated two inches. "Bailey told me that one of the former employees accidentally fell in." She lowered her voice. "He was shredded in less than a minute. Not even a shoe left. The water was a blood bath."

Crandall shivered. "Well, then, maybe we should take this conversation away..." He gestured away from the shark.

"And I think that, since you have so much in common with this fellow, you two should be properly introduced." She turned toward the shark. "Malevolence, meet Crandall Morton. Crandall, Malevolence."

And she gave him a shove right into the pool. His eyes widened in horror, arms scrabbling in the air before plunging into the water. Lucy was sure she'd never seen a man move so fast in her life. He was churning up the water something fierce, screaming and grabbing for the edge.

"Help me!" he shouted.

She looked behind him, her eyes widened. "Get out, Crandall! Oh, I can't watch!" Her fingers were splayed as they covered her eyes, leaving spaces for her to peek through.

He launched himself from the pool and looked behind him. The poor nurse shark was in the farthest corner near the bottom. She was doubled over in laughter. When she heard a male echo of that laughter, she looked over to see

Chris sharing it with her. Their gaze and smiles held for a moment before he gave her the okay sign. Even Bailey was guffawing from near the aquarium house.

Rivulets of water ran down Crandall's expensive clothing, and he shook out his leather shoes. "Okay, fine. You got your revenge." He glanced back at the shark. "That thing isn't dangerous at all, is it?"

She shrugged. "Must be full, lucky you. But I happen to know that the sawfish has not been fed yet this morning, and if you don't leave the premises this moment, I will introduce you to him as well."

"Lucy, you're making a big mistake. You won't get another offer like this one, I promise you." With a stiff gait, he walked toward the entrance.

"I know all about your offers. I'd rather keep it than sell to you."

CIVILIZATION. Lucy walked around the hotel lobby after freshening up. She should have stayed here all along, but there was the business with her father's apartment to clear up. Now she could relax in the style in which she'd become accustomed.

She thought about inviting Chris there for dinner, but somehow knew he wouldn't feel comfortable in a place where the employees wore uniforms and called you ma'am and sir. But this was where she belonged.

It reminded her that she hadn't spoken to her mother since her arrival. Of course, she'd made the expected "I'm here and alive" call. Lucy sighed, feeling responsibility weighing on her.

It was early for dinner, but she went into the dining room and ordered a shrimp salad and glass of wine. No more thoughts of Chris, she commanded herself. It was ridiculous, thinking about him as though she were a silly teenager. What was this, a *crush*? Absolutely, positively not. Thirty was too old for crushes. What she wanted was a stable man who could fill her life with fun and purpose, who understood wanting the finer things in life. What she didn't need was a fling to distract her.

Later, she stretched out on a clean, solid bed and dialed her mother. "Hi, Mother. It's Lucy."

"Darling, I thought you'd been carried off by a tribe of islanders or something."

She smiled, until the vision of one particular islander popped into her mind. "I'm fine. I've just been busy, that's all."

"Where are you staying?"

"The Island Club."

"Is it a chain? You know you should stay at chains when you're abroad, darling. It's safer."

"It's beautiful down here, Mother."

"And did your father live in a tent or hut? I always pictured him living in something like that."

She grinned, knowing her mother would bring up Sonny so quickly. "No, he lived in an apartment building. Nothing you'd ever deign to even go inside, but it wasn't all bad."

"And what about this park he traded the sailboat for? Tom said it was huge and very profitable. I find that hard to believe, knowing Sonny as I did."

"Well, Tom might be exaggerating a little." The shame of her lie returned to warm her face. "Actually, I exaggerated a bit. It's a small park, but the property is right on the water, and I've already had one offer on it. I'm working on another one."

"Well, at least you'll get something out of that deadbeat."

She wanted to tell her about the picture and newspaper articles Sonny had, but Carol would never see him as anything but a deadbeat loser. "The park, as property anyway, is worth a nice bit of money. But I'm glad I came down here. I needed the vacation. And I'm going snorkeling tomorrow."

"Snorkeling? Isn't that where you put on that ghastly mask and breathe through a tube that sticks out of the water?"

"Pretty much. Oh, and you wear fins, too." She glanced at the pile of snorkeling equipment sitting on a chair.

"Darling, it sounds dangerous. You're at least going with a licensed snorkeling captain, aren't you?"

Lucy grinned. "I'm going with a guy who grew up around the water. And he's a licensed scuba diver."

"Wait a minute, young lady. Did you say *a* guy? As in one?"

"Yes, that would be singular. Don't worry, he's quite safe. His name is Chris, and he takes custody of captive dolphins and repatriates them to the wild. He spends his life saving dolphins."

Her mother had this sound she made that usually went with seeing hippies or the like. "You're not attracted to this man, are you? Island romances sound good, in theory, but they're just not practical. I raised you to be sensible."

She twisted the phone cord. "I'm going snorkeling with him, that's all. Besides, he's not my type. I mean, he touches fish for a living, never stays in one place long, doesn't make any money."

"Lucy," Carol said, drawing out the word. "It sounds like you're trying to convince yourself more than me. Honey, I know women have...well, you know, urges when they're not married. Maybe you could try one of those...devices I've heard some women talking about. That would be much safer than a tryst."

Lucy could not believe her own mother was suggesting she use a vibrator. She decided not to comment on it. "You know, Mother, you assume all I want from this guy is a fling. What if I wanted more? What if I was, say, in love with him?"

"Lucy Annabelle Donovan, do *not* tease your mother!" She took a quick breath. "I raised you better than that. You'd never fall for a man who couldn't give you the life you deserve."

"You married a man like that."

"That was different."

"Why, because you were in love?"

"No. I mean, I was in love with Sonny, but I was young and naive. I didn't know what I wanted, and Sonny fed the silly, romantic side of me. I realized that side didn't live in nice homes with quality cars and respect. The side of me that wanted the good life overrode the silly side, and you see where I am now. Your sister is struggling because she married an artist. She followed her romantic notions, and look what it got her."

"Love?" Nancy always looked happier than Lucy ever did, even when Lucy was married.

"And not much else. Lucy, you're a good girl and I know your head is firmly on your shoulders. Call me when you get home. Bye, love."

She was still mulling over her thoughts when she found herself downstairs getting into a cab, when she found her mouth telling the driver to take her to the park, even when she found her mouth smiling as she spotted the moped parked out front. Of course, she'd just been kidding about falling in love with him. To be sure.

9

THE SUNSET PAINTED the sky shades of crimson and purple. All of those colors were reflected in the ocean, made into a living thing as the surface undulated with the earth's rhythms. Lucy took a deep breath, drawing it in, wanting to hold the sense of peace inside herself forever. She quietly unlocked the gate and slipped inside.

It was a minute before she heard the music, but she knew she'd unconsciously felt it from the beginning. Chris was only a silhouette against the sky as he sat by Liberty's pool playing his guitar.

She stood there for a long time absorbing a scene that would live in her heart for the rest of her life. She collected the smells, the sounds and every color to paint her mental snapshot.

His back was toward her as he played a song she didn't recognize at first, but touched her all the same. With every strum of his fingers against the strings, she felt the music sink deeper into her soul. It was as though Chris and Liberty were in a glass globe, something precious and not quite real.

Liberty was the only audience Chris was aware of. He was only a few inches away from Chris, and he seemed just as mesmerized as she felt. She watched, feeling as though her heart bobbed along with the swells beyond, lifting up to tighten her chest. Chris's damp curls moved slightly over his tan skin as he softly sang the words to Crosby, Stills and Nash's "The Southern Cross."

At that moment, Chris and Liberty were of the same species, and she was the outsider. She was experiencing the rare privilege of watching an exquisite moment of nature, of communication, trust and friendship. She had been drawn into their world, touched by them and by Chris's mission to save the dolphins.

Her heart tightened again, dazzled by the diamonds of the sunset sparkling over the water, and by Chris himself. He was a loner, at one only with the ocean and the dolphins. No one else had truly touched his heart. Perhaps no one had been allowed close enough to see how touching his heart was like trying to find buried treasure...illusive, hard work, and heartbreaking. Certainly dangerous for a woman like herself to even be thinking about.

But she was thinking about it.

Chris finished the song, but he plucked at one string, letting the note hang in the air like a fine mist. Liberty moved closer still. Her fingers touched her lips, holding back the sound that wanted to escape. But it was Liberty who gave her away. He caught the movement and turned toward her. Chris turned also.

"Now you're the one sneaking up on people."

She could only nod. Then her senses gained foothold and she shook her head. "I didn't mean to sneak up on you. I'm sorry."

"No problem."

He set the guitar down and stood. She moved away, not trusting herself to be near him.

"Are you all right, Lucy?"

She looked everywhere but at him, not wanting him to

read anything in her eyes. "I'm fine. I just...forgot something at the office."

When his hands touched her arms, she felt a warm rush engulf her. "You sure you're all right? You look skittish. Crandall been bothering you?"

"No, nothing like that." She looked up into his eyes, green as an inviting, warm sea. Big mistake. The babbling began. "I talked to my mother earlier, told her I was going snorkeling with you tomorrow. Not a good idea." She shook her head, long exaggerated movements. "She's all worried now."

"Does she think a shark is going to eat you?"

A nervous laugh escaped her throat. "No, she's worried about you, actually. She's worried that I might have a fling with you, you know, one of those island things, or worse, I might fall in love with you, but I told her I was too sensible for that." Good grief, she sounded like Vicki now, going on and on.

He pulled her closer, his fingers still closed over her arms. She could feel the hardness of his body pressed lightly against her own. "Are you worried about that?"

Another silly, nervous laugh. "No, of course not. I mean, we're so different. It's ridiculous, don't you think?"

He looked at her for a moment, one of those soul-probing eye-connection things that sent tickling sensations racing through her. His gaze shifted to her mouth, and his fingers tightened. His eyes found hers again, his head lowered slightly. Her heart was hammering a beat: kiss me, kiss me, kiss me. As though he could hear her, he lowered his mouth to hers. She felt her knees give and locked them into place. He was kissing her, and she was lost. His tongue grazed her lips, and she opened her mouth to him. He took the invitation and swept into her mouth. He kissed like he did everything, slow and easy. His tongue laved hers before exploring the rest of her mouth. Before she could get nearly enough, he finished the kiss and backed away.

"Who is Lucy?"

His question jarred her out of her sensual haze. "What?"

"Who is Lucy? You know about me. Tell me who Lucy is."

She moved out of his hold and ran her hand over her mouth. "So, we're not kissing anymore?"

"Nope."

"Well, it was probably a bad idea to begin with."

"Definitely."

"Positively."

"So, back to my question...who is Lucy?"

"I...well, part owner of a successful advertising agency."

"And?"

She realized she could talk all night about her agency, but talking about herself was different. "I worked very hard to get where I am. I *am* sensible and driven and a perfectionist."

He seemed to be weighing whether she was telling the truth or not. All of that was true; what else could he be looking for?

"I want you to think about what you just said. If that's all you think you are, then maybe you don't even know yourself."

"Of course I know who I am."

He touched the tip of her nose, an I-know-a-secret smile on his face. "Think about it. You need a ride back to the hotel?"

"Uh, yes. I'd appreciate it." She glanced at the office. "Guess I'd better get that...thing I forgot."

She found something viable and met him by the pool. He was stroking Liberty's wet skin, and the dolphin looked as though he were in heaven. She knelt down beside him.

"Can I touch him?" she asked.

"Let me see your hands."

She raised them. "They're clean."

"I'm not looking for dirt." He ran his fingers over the tips of her nails. She hoped he didn't catch the shiver at his touch. "You can't touch him with nails like this."

She looked at her manicured nails with rounded edges and a sensible pink polish. "They're too sharp?"

"Dolphin skin is so sensitive, even smooth nails can scratch." He held up his own hands, nails trimmed short and neat. "This short."

"I'll have to think about that." She glanced at the guitar. "Liberty likes music?"

"Yeah, especially when you prolong the sound of a chord. It makes me wonder if we could somehow communicate with them through music. And then I start thinking of how that could be done, what instrument would we use and it boggles my brain."

He stood and led the way to the gate. She wanted to suggest a drink at Barney's, but she felt overwhelmingly vulnerable and afraid she'd do something foolish like throw herself at him or even possibly cry. His question about who she really was echoed uncomfortably in her mind. Instead, she held on tight as they rode to The Island Club.

When she got off the bike, she found herself saying, "Would you like to have a drink in the bar?"

He looked up at the elegant entrance and shook his

head. "Not my style, Miz Lucy." He reached up and pushed a lock of hair away from her cheek. She swayed toward him for a kiss, but he said, "Good night."

And then he was gone. She walked into the lobby and up to her room.

Who was Lucy? She sat on the balcony overlooking the pool and thought of her responses. Owner. Sensible. Practical. Driven. Perfectionist. She'd left out successful, competitive, divorced. Who was she outside of work? She came to a startling realization: everything she was was wrapped around her professional life.

Her accomplishments were artistic, creative and important. But had they made a difference? Not really. Not freeing people or dolphins or anything. Not healing souls.

So, who was Lucy?

She took it down to the basics. She was a woman. Deep inside, she was a romantic, too. She kept that part hidden, but down here it came out. Here she was that romantic, lonely woman who wanted more of that kiss. Who needed it. Okay, now she was stripping herself bare, and she didn't much like it.

She leaned against the balcony and watched people enjoying the good life. That was what life was about.

Tomorrow she would tell Chris she was a woman who was happy with her life, and that's all that mattered.

THE NEXT MORNING Chris watched Lucy walking around the different pools toward him and Liberty, a strange but pleasant feeling warming him from the inside out. Her brown hair swung with her steps, and yesterday's pink had turned to a light brown that tipped her nose and cheeks. She carried the old duffel bag with the snorkeling gear they'd found yesterday. She, of course, wanted to wash and probably disinfect it.

"Good morning," she said, setting down the bag.

"Hi."

Liberty popped out of the water and emitted clicking noises, making Lucy laugh. My, but she had a nice laugh and a smile that produced more of that feeling inside him. It had been so hard not to continue that kiss.

"Good morning to you, too, Liberty," she said, sitting down on the edge of the pool. She lifted her hands to show short, albeit polished nails. "I want to touch him."

He couldn't help wishing it was him she wanted to touch. He shivered at the specific image of those fingers around one particular body part. Liberty had already ducked back into the water and circled, pausing to check out the speakers Chris had just put on the bottom. He walked through the water toward her, finding a flowery scent that tickled his nose. He took her hands and ran his palms over the edges.

"Okay, you're cleared for touching. Take your hands and slap them gently on the surface of the water like this."

He demonstrated, and she followed suit. Liberty zig-zagged through the water toward her, making her laugh again. He popped his head out of the water directly in front of her.

"I think he has a crush on you," Chris said.

She twisted her mouth. "I'm not the kind of woman people—or animals—have crushes on."

"So you say." He purposely averted his gaze to Liberty. "Go ahead. You know you want to give her a kiss." He made a gesture with his hands, something he'd read in the training book.

Her eyes widened as Liberty used his flukes to move

closer to the edge and pressed the tip of his snout to her cheek. She touched the wet spot and straightened, a look of awe on her pretty face.

"He *kissed* me!"

"Well, if I'd known that's all it takes to excite you..."

She looked over at him, eyebrows raised. "Are you flirting with me?"

"Nah." He shook his head to emphasize the point. But he *was* flirting with her, and he was in a damned good mood for a change.

Chris pulled himself up out of the water next to her. "There's a small fishing tribe called Imragen on the edge of the Sahara Desert. They rely on their winter catch of mullet, and they keep sentries posted to spot the schools as they pass by. When they see one, the tribesmen all run to the water and beat the surface with sticks. The dolphins hear the sound from far away and come to chase the mullet into their nets near the shore. In the bargain, they get to eat the escapees." He looked at Liberty's gray form beneath the water. "Man and animal working together."

"That's incredible." She was looking at him as though he'd done something great. "You love what you do, don't you?"

"Sometimes I love it, and sometimes I hate it. This part I love, working with a dolphin who's going to go free, making progress. Most of my time I'm writing letters, making phone calls, fighting with government agencies or other entities."

She kept looking at him with a kind of compassion that went right to his gut. "You know what I think?"

"Uh-oh, this sounds philosophical."

"Brace yourself—it is. I think healing these dolphins' souls helps you heal, too. You look out for them because you didn't have anyone to look out for you when you were a kid. Am I right?"

He sat there for a moment, letting her words wash over him. He'd never looked at it like that. "Maybe you're right, Miz Lucy. Maybe you're right."

As long as her hand was in the water, Liberty shortened his circles to touch her more frequently. She looked mystified each time he slid by her fingers.

"He feels sort of like an inner tube," she said, smiling as he passed by again.

"Yeah, a bit."

As she leaned forward, he caught a glimpse of a creamy curve of flesh beneath her tank top. He found himself wanting to rub up against her, but squelched the thought before his body could take note of it. She wasn't an island girl looking for a fling. Lucy had class, and there was a lot more to her than the exterior. She was the kind of woman a man wanted to make his wife, a woman to take out to fancy restaurants and the theater and have a picture of on his desk. Yep, that's the kind of woman she was. And he wasn't the kind of man to give it to her.

As though she'd somehow read his thoughts, she turned to him and said, "You want to know who Lucy Donovan is? She's a woman who's accomplished a lot, who has lived up to her expectations and is...happy with her life."

Something didn't quite ring true with the last part of that statement, but he nodded anyway. "That's what matters, Lucy. That you're happy."

"I am. I'm really, very happy. Most people would be, you know. A beautiful apartment, successful business, loads of money and, if I look hard at myself in the mirror, I'm okay looking." A thread of desperation slivered through her voice. "I have everything I want. And I'm young. I have a lot more to look forward to."

"Sure you do."

She shrugged. "I'm a little lonely sometimes, but that's because I work so much. That's what you have to do to be successful these days. And I'm fine with that, you know? I'm very happy," she said again, nodding her head. "I couldn't be happier." She looked at him, and that phony smile faded before she dropped her forehead to her knees. "I'm such a liar."

He wasn't sure what to say. He wanted to reach out and put his hand on her shoulder, but he stopped himself.

She lifted her head, her forehead pink where her knees had pressed against it. "I haven't told anyone this. I recently turned thirty. That has to be it. It's just that I feel..." She tried to express it with her hands, twirling her fingers in front of her. "Empty. And I feel really bad for feeling that way. I have everything. People respect me." She narrowed her eye at him. "Well, *most* people."

"I respect you."

"You do?"

"Sure. You have accomplished a lot. Why do you feel empty?"

"I wish I knew." She dipped her fingers in the water. "I haven't told anyone how I feel because they'd probably laugh at me. My mother would send me packing to her favorite psychiatrist of the month. Happiness is success to my parents. No one would understand." She glanced at him. "You, least of all, so I don't know why I'm telling you all this."

"I've been there."

"You have?"

"Sure. When I was head trainer at Aquatic Wonders, I

enjoyed my work and had the rapt attention of young women during every show. The money wasn't bad, either. It still wasn't enough."

She sighed, shifting her attention to Liberty. "But you had the dolphins. They were in your heart and soul." She shook her head. "I can't imagine giving it all up. People would think I was crazy."

"Ah, they did. Lucy, you're not made to give up what you've worked hard for. You're going through a phase."

She looked hopefully at him. "You think so?"

He found himself reaching out before he could pull back. His fingers grazed her chin. "Sure. You turned thirty. Losing your twenties is a big shakeup for some people. You'll find yourself a boyfriend, get married, have a family and you'll be right back in the groove."

She didn't look convinced. "The Great Green Lie."

"If it works for you."

"I'm not in any hurry to get married again. Not after Tom."

"What was wrong with Tom?" He found himself curious about her life. Who was Lucy? He wanted to know. Not the businesswoman, but the woman inside.

"Oh, Tom's perfect. Good-looking, ambitious, has it together. We met in college. We had a storybook wedding and a textbook marriage. But he resented the fact that it was my family who gave us the money to open our business.

"And so started the competitiveness within our marriage. He worked long hours, so he expected me to. All we ever talked about was the business. I got caught up in the whole thing with him, bringing in the biggest clients, the most money. And when one of my campaigns won an industry award, he got even worse."

He shook his head. "I thought marriages were supposed to be partners working together, not against each other."

"I grew up that way, but you're right, it shouldn't be that way in a marriage. I wanted the romance thing. You know, like the scene in the movie, *An Officer and a Gentleman* when Richard Gere carries Debra Winger out of that factory? That's what I wanted. What I got was a business partner who happened to share the same bed. And barely that. We've been divorced for a year now, proud of ourselves for being so polite and civilized, keeping the business going. But he's hinting that I'm not doing my fair share. I look at him now and wonder what I ever saw in him. What my parents wanted, maybe? Who knows? I'm tired of him, tired of the snide comments, all of it." She looked over at him. "Why am I telling you all this? Now you probably lost that little shred of respect you had for me."

"I think I actually respect you more. Miz Lucy, you're a lot different than I thought you were when we first met. I don't understand you and your world, but I respect you."

She gave him a wry smile. "Thanks. I think."

He stood, extending a hand to her. "Come on. Help me feed Liberty. Then we'll go check the traps."

When she rose up next to him, he had the most irresistible urge to hold her. She was something, all right. Strong, vulnerable, compassionate and a little lost. If only untraining her was the same as untraining a dolphin.

His fingers were still holding hers lightly, and he squeezed them. She looked up at him, her eyes full of things he couldn't begin to comprehend. He felt that strange tightness in his chest and took a deep breath. *Don't get attached, Maddox. It ain't worth it.*

She licked her lips, and he knew if he didn't move away, he'd kiss her. He could almost taste her lips on his as he wrenched away. "We'd better get going," he said, surprised at how gruff his voice was.

Behind him, he could hear her faint voice say, "I think we almost were."

10

"TELL ME ABOUT Bailey's friend's deal," Chris asked as he pulled nylon bags from his duffel at The Caribe Plantation's boathouse.

Lucy loved the way the muscles in his arms moved, loved the way his whole body moved actually. Everything was one fluid motion made by a lean, hard body.

"Well, his friend wants to put up some villas. Nothing fancy, more for families on budgets. He's in the States on business, so I spoke with him on the phone. He seems like a nice guy. Not like Mr. Slick," she said with a laugh. "He's not offering me as much money, though. And I'll have to hold the note, though I'll earn interest that way. I have to give it some thought."

He straightened, holding a nylon bag with his equipment in it, along with the empty bags for the fish. "Ready, Jackie Cousteau?"

Her throat tightened, but she nodded. "Ready."

They walked down the boardwalk, and she eyed the dark shapes that seemed to move beneath the current in the distance. "Are you sure those things aren't creatures over there?"

"I told you, they're reefs. Don't forget, you can't touch the coral, because they're delicate and can die."

"Believe me, I don't plan on going around touching things down there." Except maybe him. She'd like to touch him.

After going over underwater signals, he asked, "Sure you don't want to chicken out?"

"Positive. Let's go."

He was already in that little swimming-trunk thing, but she wasn't about to wander around in her bathing suit until she was ready to go into the water. She took off her shirt and shorts, feeling naked in her high-cut one-piece. She'd already bared her soul to the man; what was a little skin between them now?

He was squinting in the sun, giving her an appreciative, low whistle. "The advertising princess has a figure."

"You don't know how to give a straight-out compliment, do you? I know, you flunked chivalry," she said when he started to respond.

"Don't forget it," he said with a playful smile as he helped her adjust her mask and snorkel.

"How can I?"

"Ready to plunge?" he asked, putting his equipment in place.

"Ready," she answered in a muffled voice that echoed through the snorkel tube.

"Stay close to me."

Like that would be a problem, she thought. They both did a shallow dive into the water. He even moved like a dolphin, fluid strokes using his whole body. They swam through a gateway of coral reefs that opened to the ocean beyond. Way ahead it looked dark blue and eerie as it got deeper. Luckily he turned to the left along the edge of the crust of reef separating the boathouse from the open ocean.

His fins swished past her, sending a warm current of water washing over her face. The muscles in his legs flexed, and the tiny hairs danced in the water, making her grin for some reason. *Lucy, you're supposed to be noticing the ocean life!*

He grabbed her hand and pointed ahead where a large sea turtle scurried away from them and toward that deep blue abyss. He squeezed her hand before letting go, and even with the glass of the masks between them, she could feel the warmth of his smile.

He pointed toward the coral and moved closer, hovering above the intricate mass of color. It was its own universe, filled with life-forms that looked alien and beautiful. He took her hand, gave her the swirl signal and down they went. A thin fish the size of a small pet swam along the bottom, and he headed toward it. It was black, covered with spots, with a tall fin pointing upward. They followed it, flanking either side until it got spooked enough to ditch them.

"What was that?" she asked when they reached the surface.

"A French angelfish. Check this out, but stay at the surface."

She watched him swim down to something buried in the sand next to the reef. He touched it, and a stingray lifted from its cloak of sand and seemed to fly away. Now she knew why he loved it down here so much. Everywhere she looked, there was something wondrous and new.

After a while, they wended their way back to the shallow section. She'd never felt so exhilarated in her life. She pulled off her mask and slung it over her arm, yanked off her fins and planted her tired legs in the sand. Sunshine winked everywhere around her, dancing on the waves, but she was more dazzled by the man who sprang up in front of her.

"It's incredible down there! You're right—it's a lot different seeing them in their environment than in the tanks." She didn't know what was more important, catching her breath or telling him how wonderful the world he'd opened up to her was. "I want more." Her eyes met his. "I want to see all of it."

He had the most gorgeous grin as he took her in, and she yearned to touch his chin, just once. "It's addicting down there."

"You should have warned me." *He* was addicting, sneaking up on her heart by doing nothing more complicated than playing the guitar for a dolphin. No, it was more than that. It was him, what lived in his heart and soul, what he lived for. "I'll never forget this."

"Yes, you will. You'll go back to your life and forget all about us."

She looked right into his eyes. "Never."

His hands came up to brace her cheeks, and his thumbs rubbed over two spots on either side of her mouth.

"Please don't tell me I have seaweed sticking to my cheeks," she said.

He studied the two spots. "You know, you've got the sweetest dimples I've ever seen."

"I don't have dimples. Maybe they're wrinkles."

He shook his head. "Nope, they're dimples. Not very deep, and they only show when you really smile like you were doing. Or when you watch Liberty."

"I have dimples?"

"Yep."

He held her face, looking into her eyes and taking her breath away all over again. Her smile faded away to something bare and naked inside her, a question, a yearning. He pulled her closer and gently kissed one supposed dimple, then the other. Now she really couldn't breathe. And then he touched his wet lips to hers.

A sound rumbled deep in her throat, something she'd never heard before. She closed her eyes and savored the feel of his mouth moving over hers, tasted the salt as her mouth opened to his. Warmth rushed from the tips of her toes to her cheeks. Her feet were sinking in the sand. A slight breeze washed over her wet skin, but nothing could cool the fire burning within her.

His hands left her cheeks to pull her flush against his body. He wanted her, and his body had no qualms about letting her know. The tightness in her chest spread to her outer limbs. She wanted him, too. Gracious, she wanted him. Her hands went to his shoulders, sliding into the damp curls at his neck. His tongue made liquid love to hers, moving against hers in slow, rolling motions that coincided with the incoming waves.

She didn't want this to end yet. She didn't want to leave tomorrow. Six nights wasn't enough. Six years wasn't enough. What was she thinking? *No, don't think, Lucy. Just feel. For once in your life, feel.*

Chris let out a long sigh and finished the kiss. He looked at her for a moment, then pulled her close again and rested his chin on top of her head. The fingers of one hand trailed up and down her back while the other held her against his chest.

"Tell me about your life in St. Paul, Lucy," he said at last, resignation in his voice.

She looked up at him, finding something hazy in his green eyes. "My life in St. Paul?"

He leaned down and kissed her again, drawing her far, far from St. Paul. Keeping his mouth close to hers, he murmured, "Tell me about your day. What you do, how you come up with ideas."

When she tried to meet his eyes to see what he was thinking, she saw that they were closed. "Why do you want to know all that...*now?*"

He kissed her again, afterward remaining nose against nose, forehead against forehead. "Because I want to remember that you're going back tomorrow, that you belong somewhere else."

She drew in a breath, which he cut off by kissing her again. She wanted to forget about tomorrow, about belonging anywhere else but here in his arms. This wasn't supposed to hurt, but oh, it did. Deep inside it started, spreading from her heart to taint every part of her.

"I can't think of anything," she whispered, moving slightly to kiss him again.

"Then make something up." Another kiss, and the sound of his breath coming faster.

"Maybe I could extend my stay a few days," she said, but shook her head as reality set in. "No, damn it, I can't. I've got so many meetings set up this week." Meetings, the office, everything seemed so unreal to her now. This was real, this place, this man. She looked up at him, and he opened his eyes. "I want to stay."

He tipped her chin up. "But you can't. And you shouldn't. You've got a business to run. That's your life." He glanced around. "This is an interlude, something to take your mind off the world for a while. When you get back, you'll be so wrapped up in your life, this will seem like a dream. You'll be sitting at your desk and think of some incident. You'll smile at the memory, and then you'll wonder if it was a memory. Did all this actually happen? Maybe, and maybe not."

"I'm not going to forget."

His smile was tinged with the cynicism she knew too well. "Everything fades into the quilt work of yesterday.

We can't hold on forever." He reached out and touched her cheek, and she leaned into his palm. "Miz Lucy, I'm relieved to know that there is still some good in the world." His thumb rubbed over her lower lip. "You are quite a lady."

His words swirled inside her, quelling the ache a little. "Coming from you, I take that as a big compliment, being good and all." But was she good? Had she done anything important in her life? Something that mattered to someone other than herself? She didn't share her doubts, relishing his praise and not wanting to make him question it.

He widened his eyes. "Do you know what we forgot to do?"

"Check the traps for fish," they both said simultaneously.

They traded a sheepish look, and she laughed. "Oops. I got so caught up in the sea life, I forgot."

He lifted an eyebrow. "And I got so caught up in the rare St. Paul mermaid, I forgot, too. Come on, let's get Liberty's dinner. And maybe something for us."

She had never had such a wonderful time. And she had never felt about a man the way she felt about Chris. She let out a long sigh and, grabbing up her fins, followed him to shore.

How could she have let this happen?

11

BACK AT THE PARK, Lucy went to the restroom while Chris put the fish in the big cooler. She stared at her reflection in the mirror, tilting her head and smiling. No dimples, just as she'd thought. Maybe he was making it up. She tried to think about what they'd been doing when he'd remarked upon them. She'd been telling him she would never forget him or Liberty. Warmth spread over her, and she watched the amazing appearance of...dimples. Didn't she ever smile like this? Her eyes sparkled with a dreamy quality, and for that moment she looked quite beautiful. She stopped smiling. She wasn't supposed to look that happy, not with Chris.

Liberty was a happy camper when he saw them approaching. Just as she was going to ask for a fish to feed Liberty, Chris handed her one. Their gazes caught for a moment, an understanding, a bond that extended to Liberty.

"I'm varying his feedings so he gets out of a schedule." He tossed a fish on the far side of the pool, then one at the other end. "Soon I'll stop feeding him directly. He won't know where the fish are coming from."

She felt a little sad when the bucket was empty. The end. They'd started out with eight pounds of fish and now it was gone. Seven days in the Bahamas had seemed like a long time, too, but now it was almost gone.

"Do you miss them when they go free?" she asked.

"The dolphins?"

"Yes. You spend a lot of time with them."

"I go in knowing they're going to leave. I suppose I miss some of them, but I'm happier knowing they're free." His fingers tightened over her hand.

"Bye, Liberty," she said, feeling an emptiness at even his loss.

As THE SUN began its descent, Chris cooked a couple of yellow-tailed snappers he'd taken from the traps, and they ate on the beach. They talked about trivial things, anything but the somber mood that underscored the evening. Lucy remembered the camera she'd brought, and wandered around taking pictures while Chris lay back on the blanket.

"Did you take a picture of me?" he asked when she joined him a few minutes later.

"Yes. Do you mind?"

"I don't think so. But why did you take it?"

She leaned forward until their faces were only inches apart. "I don't want to forget you."

He looked at her for a moment, as though he couldn't fathom why she would want to capture him forever. Then he leaned forward and kissed her.

"Stay with me tonight, Lucy."

Her chest tightened at his words, but she didn't hesitate in her answer. She'd been hoping he'd ask, afraid to suggest it for fear of rejection. The smile with the dimples spread over her face. "I'd love to."

She reached out and touched his chin, running her fingers along the bottom edge and over the slight stubble. He kissed her again, long and slowly, awakening every nerve in her body. Warmth pooled in her lower stomach, then lower yet. How long had it been since she'd felt this way…felt like a woman?

"Do you want to take a shower?" he asked.

Another flush washed over her body. "W-with you?"

He grinned. "That was the idea. Chicken?"

"Chicken! No way."

Absolutely way. Her stomach quivered as he led her to the boathouse. There were parts of her—deep, feminine parts—that ached at the thought of being touched by Chris. She was chicken, but she wasn't going to chicken out.

"You're going to need clothes," he said.

"I've got an extra shirt in my bag. In fact, I've still got your shirt." She didn't want to give it back.

He shrugged. "Keep it if you want."

She smiled despite herself and her intention to make light of his gift. "Thanks."

He looked at her again in that questioning way as though he couldn't understand why she'd want something as silly as his shirt. She couldn't even explain it to herself.

The sunset washed everything in pink-and-gold tones, even Chris's skin. He looked at her before disappearing around the corner. He was leaving it up to her. Like she really had a choice. She moved forward, pulling off her shirt as she turned the corner and found him standing there. Her heart stopped beating.

He stood naked beneath the water as it sluiced down the muscles and tan skin of his body. He reached out to her, his long fingers beckoning her forward.

Her fingers slid against his wet ones as he pulled her closer. Their bodies barely touched as they stood beneath the cool water. He slid his finger beneath the strip of her bathing suit, dislodging one strap and then the other. She started to pull the rest down, but he stopped her with nothing more than a look. Very slowly he ran his fingers beneath the top of her suit, making her breasts tingle with warmth. He took his time working her suit down, taking in every inch of her like she were some magnificent sea creature to cherish.

His hands skimmed down her bare waist, rolling the suit over her hips until it dropped down to her feet where she stepped out of it. She wanted to touch him, to feel him against her, but he ran his hands back up her hips, over her stomach to the curves of her breasts. His thumbs circled the sensitive skin until she thought she might die of wanting him. Blindly she reached out, placing her palms against his chest, too distracted to inflict the same sweet torture on him.

She rolled her head back, eyes closed, and let out a long, low moan. He pulled her flush against him, matching her sound with a growl that vibrated from his mouth directly to hers as he kissed her. His hands slid over the wet curves of her back and bottom, pulling her closer yet. She felt him pressing hard against her stomach, felt his skin against her sensitized breasts. Her hands explored down his sides where she felt the ridges of his ribs, the smoothness of his waist and the slimness of his hips.

He tilted her head back and slid his tongue beneath her chin and nibbled at her neck. Reaching behind her, he took the bottle of shampoo and poured some out, lathering it into her hair, never once moving more than half an inch away. Bubbles slid down her chest to collect where their bodies fused together. She poured a dollop of shampoo into her palm and did his hair next, relishing the feel of his curls twining around her fingers.

The liquid soap was next. He stepped back for the first time since he'd pulled her close and slid his soapy hands over every curve of her body, over and over and over until her knees threatened to collapse into jelly. This was what she'd been dreaming about the last time she'd showered here. She grabbed for the soap and turned the tables, realizing why he'd taken so long, relishing the pleasure of feeling every contour, even the ones that made his fingers close tightly over her waist.

He moved them to the shower, kissing her beneath the flow of water as it washed over them and collected in the basin. She could vaguely hear the *drip drip* as it overflowed and drizzled down beneath the boards to splash into the water below.

He reached behind her to turn off the water, pressing her back against the wall in the process. His chest was rising and falling heavily, touching her slightly with each exhalation. His hands were planted on either side of her, and his face so close she could feel a drop of water transfer from his nose to hers.

She whispered, "I'm not the kind of woman who... partakes in...one-night stands, you know."

"I know." He kissed her again, a slow, sensual kiss. "But you know that's all this would be, don't you? All it can be?"

His words stung, but she knew he was right. "I know." But didn't he dare entertain thoughts of forever?

"Lucy?" he asked in a raspy voice. "Are you sure this is what you want?" He was looking into her soul again, seeing the sensible Lucy that had been forgotten in the last few days. "You're leaving tomorrow, back to your life and your business. And from here, I go on, too. I don't want you hurt."

She was trying not to think about all that, but he was right. This was a one-night stand, a vacation fling. She wasn't a fling type of girl. But at that moment she wanted to be, very, very badly and she knew she'd be hurt very badly, too, when they had to part. "We could, you know, write. And call each other."

He reached up and took her chin in his hand. "Never works. Let's make it a clean break."

"You want me to leave?"

"No." The word ground out of him. "I want you to stay. I just don't want any illusions between us."

"I have no illusions," she whispered, but her heart called her a liar. Her desire went deeper than physical, warning her that making love would bring on an avalanche of heartbreak. "What if I just...sleep here?"

His finger trailed from her forehead over her nose to her lips. "Ever spent the night in a hammock with a man before?"

"Before the other night, I'd never spent the night in one period."

They dried each other off, taking their time to make sure every crevice was attended to. He tugged her arm, pulling her into the boathouse where they snuggled into the hammock together. Her fingers brushed his bracelet, that reminder about not getting attached. His desire was evident, pressing insistently against her flesh. She ached for the sacrifice he was making—and the one she was making, as well. She turned to him, their cheeks brushing.

"How do you know I'm not the one-night stand type?"

"I can see it in your eyes."

"But you've had...flings before. If I was willing, what did it matter what kind of girl I am?"

"You ask too many questions, you know that?"

"Mmm-hmm. So?" She tightened her hold on the bracelet, bringing his gaze to her fingers. "Are you afraid of getting attached to me?"

He rubbed his cheek against hers, his eyes closed. "I'm going to miss you, Lucy. That's as attached as I want to get."

She closed her eyes, too, feeling warm and tired, paradoxically satisfied and hungry at the same time. He pulled her closer, and she hooked her leg over his. Their bodies were sealed together, naked, but chaste. She didn't want to think about tomorrow, wished it would never come. And as she drifted in the netherworld between wakefulness and sleep, she knew she wanted this man more than anything in the world. And it wasn't an illusion.

LUCY COULD SEE sunlight from behind her closed eyes, but something else was there, too. She opened her eyes to find Chris watching her with a content smile. It felt like a balloon was inflating inside her, expanding her insides as she met his eyes. *I love this man.* The voice inside her stated this so unequivocally, she shivered. No, she couldn't love him.

"Cold?" he asked, pulling her closer.

She glanced down, realizing she was naked. Her hand was splayed across his stomach, as though he belonged to her. Their skin was damp wherever they connected.

"Definitely not."

She was drowning.

She looked down at her hand again, at the spray of hair that her pinky finger touched the edge of. Her leg was still slung over his lower body, discretely covering his anatomy, though she was well aware of it beneath her thigh. She moved her hand over his stomach, to his chest. He felt warm and solid. Would she ever look back on this and think it was only a dream?

He watched her, and she wondered if he could see her

inner turmoil. Now she understood clearly what he meant by a clean break. What he didn't realize was that this was not a fling nor a one-night stand. If they made love, she somehow knew it would change her, touch her and never let her go. Or maybe he did understand that. It was crazy, but some part of her actually felt as though she belonged here with him.

"I get up at five-thirty every morning," she said, taking up his earlier question. "I do some weights or a workout tape, then I get ready for work. I usually have at least three meetings, either with our art department or with clients. There are always deadlines to meet, people to please, new business to lure. It probably doesn't sound very exciting to you."

"I can't even imagine what that kind of life is like. I'm sure my life probably doesn't sound very exciting to most people."

"Actually, it sounds kind of crazy." She smiled. "And very heroic."

He smirked. "It's not heroic. It's just something I do."

And that's why she loved him. The thought sped her heartbeat. Oh, no, she *did* love him. When had it happened? It had started when he'd played the guitar for Liberty. She could never tell him she felt that way. First of all, he wouldn't believe her. She wasn't sure if she even believed it. It was crazy. She'd known him only a week, yet he had drawn her into his world. Into him.

"I wish I could stay even one more day." *I wish I could stay forever.*

"You'll feel differently when you get back to your life," he said.

"How can you be so damned sure?"

He rolled the hammock until it threatened to spill them out, then helped her to stand before joining her. "Because this is not your life. You belong in St. Paul, and as soon as you get home, you'll realize that."

She sighed. "But don't you wish—"

"Don't go there, Lucy." His seriousness quelled any hope she had that he might entertain any illusions about their future. They had none, he was telling her. He was right, of course, but it hurt that he wasn't even willing to hope they could. "What time is your flight?"

"Two o'clock."

"I'll take you to your hotel so you can pack. Come by the park to say goodbye, okay?"

She nodded, tightening her lips because she felt an insane urge to cry. "I want to take some pictures before I leave here." She grabbed her camera and walked outside before realizing she was still naked. Lord, but she'd become bohemian. She slipped back in to change before stepping out into the sunshine again.

White, fluffy clouds skittered across the vivid blue sky. No one would believe that the water really looked like glass cleaner, that whole worlds lived beneath the surface. She wanted to capture the sounds, the smells, and most of all the feelings this place gave her, even the little ache that had settled into the pit of her stomach. She realized that it had replaced the emptiness that had once resided there.

LUCY SAID HER GOODBYES to Bill and made arrangements for him and Bailey to stay on until she decided what to do with the park. Bailey was going to take her to the airport. She pulled out her camera as she approached where Chris was absorbed in that social touching thing with Liberty. Like the day he'd played guitar for the dolphin, she stood mesmerized for a moment as Chris's nose touched Liberty's snout. Then she forced herself to position the camera and take a picture.

Chris turned at the sound of the shutter releasing. "Uh-oh, more pictures."

She took another one of Liberty bobbing his head.

"So I don't forget," she said, kneeling down by the edge of the pool.

"Sometimes it's better to forget."

Would he forget her? The thought made her heart ache. She smacked the surface of the water, and Liberty swam over and popped his head up. She ran her fingers over his wet surface.

"Liberty, have a good life, you hear me? Never ever let anyone catch you again. Understand?"

Amazingly, Liberty nodded his head before submerging again.

"Should be an easy flight to Miami from here. Weather looks good."

"I was almost hoping for bad weather. Then I wouldn't have a choice but to postpone leaving."

His smile was faint, but he looked out over the water for a minute before meeting her gaze. "But eventually you'll have to return anyway."

"I know." She trailed her finger in the water, gaining Liberty's attention for a moment even though he was on the other side of the pool.

"He's using his sonar," Chris said. "Hopefully he'll reintegrate with the wild dolphins quickly."

"But will they let him in? You said he had no dolphin identity anymore."

He smiled. "You remembered that?"

"Yeah, I actually listened to you, even if you were—"

"A creep?" he supplied with a grin.

"Yeah."

Their smiles faded, turning to something more serious. It was hard to believe she'd ever felt that way about him. She turned away this time.

"They're incredible creatures," she whispered.

"That's why I do what I do."

She nodded, knowing that dolphins like Liberty needed a champion, knowing they deserved one. "Are you the only one who does this?"

"There are a few organizations that try to help the dolphins. You remember the *Flipper* series from the seventies?"

"Sure, I grew up on reruns of that show."

"Matt Adamson trained the five dolphins who played Flipper. When his favorite died of a broken heart and isolation after the show went off the air, he realized that dolphins weren't meant for captivity and weren't put on this earth to entertain us. He founded the Dolphin Project years ago. Our paths crossed when he testified to the U.S. House of Representatives on the investigation of several government agencies supposedly responsible for the welfare of marine animals." He shook his head. "Even I didn't realize how high the mortality rate was at the parks. Right now he's involved in a controversial row with the Navy over the dolphins they trained for combat in the Cold War. He went on a hunger strike in Israel and got them to ban dolphin importation." He laughed softly. "The man means business when it comes to dolphins."

"Why don't you work with him? Sounds like the two of you have a lot in common."

Chris smiled wryly. "That we're both crazy enough to throw our lives away so we can free dolphins?" He shrugged. "I've learned a lot from his studies and techniques. But I work alone. That's how I've always worked."

She nodded slowly. *Take a hint, girl. He's trying to tell you something.* But what did it matter anyway? It wasn't like she would throw her life away and join him on his quest to free dolphins. Now that would be insanity at the highest levels.

He looked at his watch. "Are you about ready to head for the airport?"

Her mouth stretched into a frown. "I guess."

He slid out of the water in the way that always amazed her. He grabbed a towel and his clothes and walked around to where she sat. "Let's go then."

"You're taking me?" Her voice lifted at the end of her question, though she dared not hope that's what he meant.

"Bailey's letting me use his car."

He changed into shorts and a cotton shirt while she said goodbye to Bailey.

She took one last look at the park. "I guess this is it," she said, turning to Chris. "Let's go."

She felt so different than the woman who had arrived at the small airport seven days ago. He found a parking spot and took one of her bags as they headed into the building. She checked in and was delighted to find him taking a seat in the waiting area.

"You don't have to stay if you don't want to," she found herself saying as she sat down next to him.

"Don't you want me to stay?"

She touched his arm. "Yes, I do. It's just what people say, you know, to be polite. I know, part of the Great Green Lie."

Too soon they announced the boarding of her flight to Miami. She and Chris stood simultaneously. They both started to say something, both stopped. She smiled, taking a deep breath.

She said, "Thank you for everything."

A man of few words, he simply pulled her close and kissed her. Afterward, he framed her face with his hands.

"Be happy, Lucy." He kissed the tip of her nose.

She wanted to get his address, or give him one of her business cards, but his words came back to her about clean breaks. To heck with clean breaks, she thought, digging in her purse and giving him a card.

"In case..." Did she even want to hope that he would write?

He looked at the card made of deep blue vellum. "I'm not much of a writer."

"That's okay." But it wasn't. He meant to leave her behind, and that just killed her.

She focused her attention on gathering up her carry-on bag. He was looking at her when she started to say goodbye. The tears began forming, but she wouldn't let him see.

"Goodbye," she whispered and turned quickly to blend with the group filtering out the door.

To look back or not to look back? If she turned and saw him watching, the tears would surely come. And if she turned to find he'd already left, she'd feel even worse. Just before she walked out of view, she paused, bit her lower lip and turned.

He waved.

She found herself wiping at her eyes before she could duck out of view and hurry toward the plane. Hers was a window seat, and she searched for any sign of Chris beyond the windows of the terminal. The sun reflected off the glass, and she couldn't tell whether he waited there or not. She wanted to believe he was there, so she waved just in case. And then she let one tear slide down her cheek.

CHRIS PRESSED his palm against the heated glass in response to Lucy's wave. Then he turned away and headed back to the car. She'd looked so sad. When he reached the car, he leaned against it as the plane roared to life. Now he could concentrate on Liberty. Lucy was a distraction—a pleasant one, but a distraction just the same.

And he was going to miss the hell out of her.

12

"YOU HAVE A FATAL CASE of tropical fever, young lady," Vicki diagnosed after looking into Lucy's eyes at lunch the following day. She leaned back in her chair, arms crossed in front of her, blond hair spilling over her shoulders.

"Is that what this is?"

Vicki narrowed her blue eyes. "You had a fling with that dolphin guy, didn't you?"

"No, I didn't have a fling." Vicki looked skeptical, as well she should. They'd been friends since college, but Lucy felt closer to her than she did to her own sisters. "Well, I didn't."

"Bull-loney. Girl, your eyes are sparkling and your cheeks are flushing big time."

"Okay, we got...close."

Vicki leaned even nearer. "How close?"

Lucy hedged, not wanting to share all the intimate details. "We took a shower together."

"Lucy!" Vicki tossed a napkin at her. "You mean to tell me you took a shower—naked, I presume—and didn't go all the way?"

"That's what I'm telling you. And you want to know what else?" Lucy enjoyed the disbelief in her friend's eyes. "We spent the night naked together in a hammock and didn't go all the way."

"What?!" Vicki's expression changed when she saw

the truth in Lucy's eyes. "Lucy, that is so damned romantic." After Lucy told her about some of her sea adventures, Vicki said, "What got into you down there?"

"I don't know, but I want it back."

"It's tropical fever, I'm telling you. You went down to paradise, fell in love—"

Lucy straightened. "What makes you say I fell in love?"

"I can see it in your eyes. Good grief, it's written all over your face. Anyway, it happens all the time on vacations like that. You're out of your element, you fall in love, then you come back to reality and realize what you've got isn't so bad after all and you can't actually *live* down there."

She felt empty at Vicki's words. "That's what Chris said. But I don't know, this feels...different."

"You'll get over it, trust me."

"I hope so." She moved the lettuce around on her plate, but hadn't eaten more than a bite. "I feel miserable and empty and lonely. All I know is I didn't feel this way when I was with him. Down there."

"Ah, you *are* in love."

"What if I am? I know I can't have him or that life. I know all of that, but I still fell in love with him. I miss him and Liberty, too. I keep wanting to call the travel agent and book a return flight."

"Going back's the worst thing you can do. Why prolong something that's going to end? Especially if ending hurts this bad already." Vicki leaned over and put her hand on Lucy's arm. "You'll get over it, hon. I mean, where could it go between the two of you? He's not going to move up here. And I certainly don't see you giving up everything and living down there helping him save dolphins."

"I know it would never work. I know I sound star-struck or something."

"It's okay to feel like that sometimes. I think it's good for the soul."

"Then tell me this, oh, wise Vicki. If it's good for the soul, why does it hurt so damned bad?"

LUCY'S EX-HUSBAND had been busy in meetings all morning, but his anticipated visit came right after she returned from lunch.

"So, the island girl is back at last," Tom said, making himself comfortable in one of her chairs. "How was it?" He did his usual annoying habit of tossing his straight blond hair off to the side with a flick of his head.

She was startled to realize he looked a bit like Crandall. "Uh, it was good."

He studied her. "You look different."

"The tan," she said.

"No, something else. You look...relaxed. Don't get too relaxed around here, Luce. We have a lot of work to do." He glanced at his watch, another annoying habit. "But I had to tell you the news. I landed the Empire Hotels account."

She picked up the stack of mail her secretary had left and started opening it. "That's great."

"Great? It's fantastic! Empire is the biggest hotel chain in the world. And they're going with me—er, with us."

She looked up and smiled. "I'm glad for you."

"I'm celebrating by buying a Porsche. And a Rolex. Heck, I deserve it."

"Good for you," she said, running the gold-plated letter opener down the seam of an envelope.

He stared at her in disbelief. "Come on, Luce, it's killing you. Admit it."

She set down the envelope. "Do you think we do anything important? Not making money, but helping people."

He lifted an eyebrow. "Making money *is* important, Luce. What's got into you?"

"I met a guy who has dedicated his life to saving dolphins. That's important." She waved at the office in general. "We don't save lives or souls or anything."

"We didn't get into the advertising business to save lives. We did it to make money, to be successful and revel in our creativity. Remember?"

She twisted her mouth. "I remember."

"Don't forget it." He glanced at his watch. "Gotta go. Ciao."

This was just tropical fever. She would get back in the groove. She would always cherish her time with Chris and Liberty, but her life was here.

Be happy, Lucy.

His words echoed through her soul. This was where her happiness was. It was time to get back into her life. That should take, oh, about a week. Then the Bahamas and all of it would really be a dream and nothing more. No problem, mon.

"You're doing *what*?" Tom asked, hands on his hips as he hovered near Lucy's desk.

"I'm going back down to the Bahamas."

"You just got back, and it's taken you two weeks to come down from the clouds. Now you're leaving again?"

She placed her hands on the desk. "I have some business to attend to."

"How long are you going to be gone?"

"I don't know."

"*What?*"

"Not overly long. Everything's taken care of as far as my accounts are concerned."

"You should be out there hustling up new accounts, not traipsing around in the Bahamas. I've been pulling more than my share of the load for a long time. I haven't complained, but now I'm speaking up."

Anger bubbled inside her. "Then why don't you buy me out?"

His eyes widened. "Luce, you don't mean that."

She stopped, startled that the words had come so easily. "No, of course I don't. I'm just tired of your insinuations that I'm not pulling my share. Maybe there are more important things than the business."

"*Nothing* is more important than the business," he ground out, finger jabbing the desk.

She shot to her feet. "And that included our marriage, didn't it, Tom? Let me tell you something...I can't live and die by this firm anymore. I love this company, and I've put my heart and soul into it from the beginning. But I need a life. I want to find someone to share that life with, someone to dream with, and I'm not ever going to do that if I live at work."

He grew silent for a moment. "Is that someone down in the Bahamas?"

"I don't know. I just have to go down there, okay? We'll talk about this when I come back."

THIS IS CRAZY. Why are you doing this? It'll never work. She hadn't let herself think of the fact that Chris had not written or called in the two weeks since she'd left. For all she knew, he had forgotten her the same way he'd predicted she would forget him. Now she was thinking about it as the cab drove her from the airport. Her heart fluttered inside as they neared the park. What if he didn't want her there? What if their whole time together meant nothing to him, and now she would be a nuisance?

She wasn't there to make a commitment or to give up her life to chase dolphin dreams with Chris. This trip was closure. One more time to experience it again and to finally say goodbye.

Bailey's car was parked to the side, along with three rental mopeds. Her heart jumped at the sight, but it wasn't where Chris usually parked. She tried hard to keep herself from running through the entrance.

"Lucy," Bill said with a smile. "What a surprise."

"Tell me about it."

She smoothed down the long, flowered skirt and tank top she'd bought on her first trip.

Chris wasn't at the pool, though it was long past noon. She ignored the dull hammering of her heart as she stepped over the chain that said Keep Away! and took the final steps to the pool. She couldn't help the sharp intake of breath—the pool was drained of every trace of water.

"No," she whispered. "He can't be gone." She had no way to get in touch with him. "Stupid, stupid, stupid coming down here without calling first," she muttered, walking back toward the office.

Bailey's musical voice drifted from the back of the park. He stood by one of the pools, gesturing as he spoke. "I caught dis giant sawfish myself," he was telling a family of pale-skinned tourists. "Nearly got my ankles cut off, but I got 'im by the back of the head and held on tight. We fought for two hours, he and I, until he finally gave up and let me take him in."

"Bailey!" she shouted from across the area.

He jerked, then had the decency to look embarrassed along with shocked at seeing her. He gave a sheepish smile to the tourists and bolted before Lucy could tell them he was full of it.

"Miss Lucy, what are you doing here? I thought you were left for good."

"Where's Chris?" she said on a rush of breath.

"He be gone."

"What do you mean, gone?"

"He take the dolphin fish and leave. He said it was time to take him outta dis place."

"So he released Liberty in the ocean and went home?"

He shook his head. "No, he take him to dat place he stay at. Me and Bill and a bunch of other guys helped him get the dolphin fish from the pool to a stretcher and den to the...Miss Lucy?"

She was already running to the road to hail a cab. Bailey caught up to her.

"You want me to take you dere?"

"Yes, take me dere—there!"

Her anticipation built again as they neared the plantation. No more disappointments, she prayed. Her heart couldn't take it. Then she saw him in the distance, waist-deep in the water where he had those nets laid out in a half moon.

"Drop me here, Bailey," she said, hopping out before he could even stop the car. She pulled out her luggage and left it behind some hibiscus bushes by the entrance.

"Sheesh, love do crazy t'ings to people," Bailey muttered, putting the car in reverse.

Love? No, it couldn't be love. She was just *in love* with Chris. And all she could think about was being in his arms again. With her heart in her throat, she ran toward the beach.

13

THE WIND RUFFLED Lucy's hair as she neared Chris. He still hadn't seen her. Being totally oblivious to everything but Liberty was nothing new. Neither was the feeling in her stomach as she took in his strong, tan shoulders that tapered to narrow hips beneath the water's surface. He was so beautiful, so wild, so everything opposite of what she wanted in life.

The doubts started again. *What if he's not happy that you came? You could leave before he sees you, save your pride before it's shattered to pieces.*

Chris held the wriggling fish out to Liberty, but the fish jerked and Liberty scooted beneath the water. She kicked off her sandals and took a step closer.

Leave now, save yourself, the voice whispered. But she couldn't move, because as though he somehow sensed she was there, he slowly turned toward her—and blinked.

"Lucy?"

She took a few steps closer to the water's edge. "Yeah." She glanced down, then up at him again.

"Is that really you, or am I hallucinating?"

She wrapped her arms around her waist. "It's me."

Then he smiled, that dazzling smile that melted right into her and let her know he was happy to see her. He washed his hands in the water and waded toward the shore. She didn't give him the chance to even reach the shallow part. She ran headlong into the water, drenching her skirt and not caring in the least.

His arms went around her, anchoring her to his body and squeezing her tighter than she'd ever been held. "Mmm, you smell so good, and you look so good, and you feel so good." He moved back a few inches, his gaze sweeping what he could see of her. "My, you look good," he said at last, shaking his head.

She leaned up and kissed his chin. "So do you."

His hair was damp and mussed, he smelled slightly of fish, and he obviously didn't believe what she'd said.

She couldn't believe she was back, and that he was happy to see her. *What am I doing? I must be crazy.* But the smile that spread across her face was nothing short of exhilarating. "Do I have dimples?" she asked, tilting her face.

He placed his thumbs on either side of her mouth. "Oh, yeah." Then he pulled her closer for a kiss, devouring her with his tongue and straddling her between his legs. When he pulled away at last, her legs could hardly hold her up. He held her steady, still looking at her with disbelief. "Why are you here?"

"I...I forgot something."

"You came all the way back because you forgot something? What could possibly be that important?"

She swallowed. "My heart."

"Oh, Lucy," he murmured, pulling her close for another kiss. When he finished the kiss, he framed her face with his hands, his thumbs moving in slow circles over her cheeks. "This is crazy."

"I know, I've been telling myself that for weeks now."

His legs brushed hers, holding them, giving them support. "Oh, girl," he said in a voice that rumbled right into her bloodstream. "You don't know what you're doing to me."

"That sentiment is mutual, believe me. My best friend thinks I'm nuts, my partner thinks I have tropical fever, and I agree with them. The only time I really smiled since I left was when I decided to come back."

"I don't care if you are crazy. I'm glad you came back. I missed you."

She felt her gaze soften as she looked in his eyes. "Did you?"

"More than I wanted to."

"Then why didn't you write or call?"

"Clean break," he said with a nod.

"You were never going to call me? Ever?"

He looked down for a moment before meeting her hurt gaze. "I honestly don't know. Maybe when my head was straighter."

Liberty brushed by her, making her jump before she realized what it was. She put her hand in the water, and he touched his snout to it.

"I went to the park, and when you were gone..." She shook her head, reliving the heartbreak again. "So this is what the nets were for."

"Yep. He's doing great. He's picking up the schools of fish swimming in the pen with his sonar, but I haven't gotten him to eat a live one yet. He's been fed dead fish for so long, live ones scare him. But he is starting to swim in straight lines instead of circles." He reached over and pulled her close. His sigh ruffled her hair. "Girl, I'm not letting you get away this time."

He meant no more near misses in the shower. His body told her body that in simple terms, understandable and agreeable to both parties.

"I had no intention of letting you get chivalrous with my heart again."

"Me, chivalrous? No way. I was protecting myself."

"Oh, I see!" He was moving them slowly toward the shore with her anchored in his arms. "And now you're not worried?"

"I don't care. I've been fantasizing about this body and this mouth ever since you left, and kicking myself for not taking advantage of you." He kissed her again. "I'd convinced myself it was for the best. And now you're back."

He wanted her. The thought slithered like a warm breeze through her body. As he neared the shore, he scooped her up in his arms, walking toward the boathouse. "You ever made love in a hammock before?"

She looked up thoughtfully, hoping he couldn't tell her heart was beating faster than bird wings. "Nope, can't say that I have."

He carried her over the boardwalk and deposited her in the hammock, not even waiting for it to stop swinging before dropping down on top of her.

"Well, then, let me initiate you."

The sun shone in the window next to them, lighting his green eyes to match the sparkling water outside. She reached up and placed her palms on either side of his face, sliding them back through his damp curls as he worked her wet skirt down. He ducked down to slide free of his swimming trunks and disappeared for a moment.

Just as she started to sit up, she felt his mouth on her toe, and then his tongue moving slowly up her calf to her thighs, and he kissed her springy hair before moving over her stomach that quivered beneath his touch. She inhaled sharply as his fingers followed the movements of his mouth, but lingered at her most private area to wend through the hair and tease what was beneath.

Her fingers anchored in his hair as he nibbled across her skin while his fingers took her right to the edge of ecstasy. She could feel the soft tip of him sliding up and down her thigh, and she was sure she'd never wanted a man the way she wanted Chris.

"Mmm." The sound escaped her mouth as she arched and drowned in waves of pleasure. He made a similar sound when she reached for him, sliding her fingers up and down the length of him in slow rhythm that coincided with the swinging of the hammock.

He lifted off her tank top, looking down at her body as though she were the most beautiful creature on earth. His hands slid over her breasts, lingering on each one in slow circles, tantalizing the stiff peaks until she was sure she'd explode. Then, agonizingly slowly, he moved down over her stomach and thighs, which he coaxed apart.

The tip of him gently prodded at her, but he hesitated when he felt resistance.

"You're tight," he said, reaching down and sliding a finger in, making her breath catch all over again.

"It's been more than a year...."

He tilted his head. "You haven't made love with anyone in more than a year?"

"Not since my ex and I got divorced."

"Oh, geez, you are sweet," he said, kneeling lower and kissing her and making her forget all those lonely nights when she didn't feel so sweet or vindicated for her virtue.

As he kissed her, his finger slid out and caressed her folds again. She didn't want to wait any longer to feel him inside her, and was about to say so...and then decided not to as pleasure curled through her body again. Her breath hitched as her chest tightened. Her toes flexed, and her fingers twined in his hair as she shuddered in pure delight. She opened her eyes and found him watching her with satisfaction. Even as waves of bliss washed over her, she pulled him close and wrapped her legs around him. He gently maneuvered in, easing into her until she felt him in every inch of her body.

"Lucy," he said between kisses, melting her with the way he said her name.

Like riding a bicycle, she thought, quickly becoming one with his rhythm. Only she was going from a tricycle to a Harley Davidson. She pulled him closer as the feelings built inside her, taking away all her trepidations about being there and making love to a man she could not have. For now, she wanted him, and that's all she knew. Then she knew nothing as white stars filled her vision and her body exploded from the inside out.

He paused, as though savoring her climax, and then his body tightened as he thrust into her once more, holding her close as a violent shiver overtook him. She clung to him just as tightly, not wanting any of this to end, ever, ever....

It was a few minutes before she could hear the sounds around them again. Birds, water lapping at the pilings beneath them, the thudding of her own heartbeat. Her eyes felt heavy, but her body felt light, floating.

He looked down at her, rubbing his fingers over her collarbone. "Lucy, you're one habit that's going to be hard to break."

He had no illusions as to why she'd come, no expectations that she'd stay. She should feel relieved, but she didn't. Of course she had no intention of throwing away her present life, and she didn't want him to think she did, but couldn't he at least wish she would?

"And I was stupid enough to think coming back

would bring closure, or get you out of my system, or I don't know what."

"This is a big mistake."

"I know."

"A really bad idea."

She sighed. "I know."

He leaned close. "I'm glad you came."

"But don't you wish—"

He kissed her silent. "Don't wish, Lucy. Just be."

"Oh, I am. Believe me, I am."

LATER THAT AFTERNOON, as the sun began looking red and gold, Lucy watched Chris from the short distance between the boardwalk and the nets. Her legs dangled over the edge, toes dipping into the water on the downward swing. If she didn't think about next week or next month or all the time beyond that, life was perfect.

"You think this is funny, don't you?" Chris said to Liberty as yet another fish escaped the fate of being dinner.

Liberty chattered happily, ready to chase another fish, and Lucy couldn't help laughing at their exchange. She loved the way Chris looked when he was concentrating, when he wanted something to work really, really bad.

He let go of another fish, and Liberty chased it all around the pen, even to the shallow end where his dorsal fin stuck way out of the water, then to the sides of the pen until the fish found a hole in the net and slipped through.

"That's it, fella." Chris held up the bucket to show Liberty that no more of those fascinating things lurked inside.

When Liberty swam over to the edge of the net nearest her, she tilted her head at him.

"Don't even look at him, Lucy."

"Not even a sympathetic look?"

"Nope, not even that. He needs to learn not to expect human interaction, response...or sympathy," he added with a wry grin as he headed toward her on the boardwalk.

She slid a sideways glance at Liberty, who was still trying to appeal to her compassion. "But it's so hard to ignore him."

"Believe me, I know it. It's all part of the untraining process. It gets even harder, when I stop talking to him altogether. Let me wash up and we'll grab a bite at Barney's."

BARNEY'S WAS HOPPING with locals, and the jukebox was nixed in favor of a live band playing what Chris told her was the native goombay music.

They sat side by side, like a regular, vacationing couple. And yet, they could never be that couple. Still, it was nice to pretend. *Geez, Lucy, that's what you're doing here, isn't it? Pretending you could make it work, pretending there aren't two major obstacles between you and him—his life and yours.*

"You're not thinking about work, are you?" he asked.

She jerked out of her thoughts, giving him a smile. "No, just thinking."

"About when you have to leave."

She gave him a surprised look. "How did you know?" When he shrugged, she said, "For someone who doesn't think much of people or hang around them, you sure know a lot about what makes them tick."

He took her hand, pressing the back of it to his mouth. "So, when are you leaving?"

"I made the return for next week, but I'm not totally against changing it. When do you think you'll let Liberty go free?"

"As soon as he starts eating live fish. I had a vet take some blood tests last week, and Liberty's free of pathogens that could kill wild dolphins. Now it's up to Liberty. When I'm sure he's able to eat on his own, I'll set him free, then keep an eye on him for another week or so before I leave. Next month I'll be back again to try to find him, make sure he's doing all right, and then again a few months later."

"I'd like to stay until you release Liberty," she said at last, when the emotion wasn't clogging her throat.

He reached out and touched her chin, taking it in a gentle hold. "I'd like that."

She couldn't help remembering their earlier encounter when he'd tried to shoo her away. He worked alone, but now he was letting her in.

WHEN THEY RETURNED to the boathouse, Chris walked down to check on Liberty, while Lucy made her way to the edge of the deck and sat facing the sun. It was a huge ball of orange fire, touching down on the horizon. He watched her silhouette, warming at the sight of her waiting for him. It was going to be hard to let her go again. He couldn't let either one of them wish for things that could never be.

He slipped on a pair of sunglasses before wading out waist-high where Liberty watched the live fish swimming around in the cage. From now on, he didn't want Liberty to make eye contact with him during feedings. It was also time to limit what he said to the dolphin. Soon Liberty wouldn't have a voice to coax him to eat.

The dolphin now sported a triangle just below the dorsal fin so that he could be tracked later. Even though Chris swore it wasn't painful, Lucy had made herself scarce during the freeze-branding process.

He leaned down to open the door. Liberty's flukes wagged in anticipation. *One more chance today. Otherwise you gotta wait until tomorrow.*

As soon as Liberty started eating live fish, Chris would start feeding him fewer dead fish. He pulled out the fish and trimmed the tail so Liberty might have a chance to catch the slower fish. Liberty touched the fish Chris held beneath the water with his snout. He didn't jump back this time.

You gonna do it for me? Come on, fella.

Chris let the fish go. Liberty chased it, and Chris held his breath as the dolphin got closer and closer. The fish was making its unsteady way toward the nets. Liberty's powerful flukes kicked in, and he reached the net a second before the fish.

And then he caught it. He seemed a little disconcerted for a moment as the fish wriggled in his mouth. He swam around and popped his head out of the water to show Chris. He wasn't moving, wasn't going to say or do a thing to interfere. And then Liberty popped the fish up in the air, caught it and swallowed it.

"Yes!" Chris shouted, pulling his fist down in victory. "You did it!"

"Did he eat one on his own?" Lucy called out. She was beautiful, washed in the hues of the sunset and looking as excited as he felt.

"He sure did. You brought us luck, Lucy."

Chris set another fish free, and Liberty made chase again before catching the mackerel.

Pretty soon no more tail trimming, fella. For now, Chris didn't want to discourage him with fish that were too quick to catch. Another mackerel went free only to be snagged by Liberty. He clicked and whistled, and Chris hoped he still remembered all of the nuances of dolphin language.

After a few more fish, Liberty was catching them easily. The last one he played with, tossing it up in the air and chasing it again once it hit the water. He was full.

Good night, Liberty, and dream of freedom. Chris headed toward the shore.

That warm, satisfied feeling filled his chest the way it always did when he claimed a victory. That feeling grew into something different when he looked toward the end of the boathouse deck.

He couldn't keep his eyes off Lucy as he walked up the boardwalk. She was sitting the same way she'd sat earlier when she'd watched him work with Liberty. Her brown hair blew in the breeze, and she sat leaning on the lower railing, resting her chin on the top edge. He quietly came up behind her, sliding his legs on either side and resting against her back.

This felt so natural, sitting there with his chin on her shoulder, and the way she turned her cheek slightly in greeting without saying a word. What would it be like, having a partner, someone to share the joys and the heartaches with? He truly couldn't imagine it, because it always had been just him, alone.

She had come back for him. He couldn't get over it, couldn't fathom that she'd left her heart with him. Even if her presence was only a tease, an interlude, he'd take it. Tasting a bit of the good of life made him remember that life was more than dolphins, and that he still had a heart beating inside him. It was a good reminder, but it wasn't going to make it any less painful when she left again.

He pointed out over the water. "Look," he said softly, as though the scene demanded some kind of reverence. For him, it did. And so it seemed, for her, too.

She sucked in a breath. "Dolphins!" She whispered the word, sensing what he felt.

Two dorsal fins rose in counter tandem, almost blending in with the choppiness of the waves. They moved closer to the pen.

"Are they here to see Liberty?" she asked, breathless awe in her voice.

"They've been by a few times, one or two of them. As soon as I put him in the pen, he started sending out signals, and this pod was nearby. I knew about the pod before I came here and had tracked their movements and numbers. I had to be sure Liberty would have a pod to join. They usually hover outside the nets. They can't discern what the net is from their signals. All they know is that it's something unnatural, but Liberty tells them not to be afraid."

"Really?" She twisted around so she could watch the two fins bobbing near the net's edge. "Should you let him go while they're here?"

"He's not ready yet. Hopefully they'll be back, but it's a chance I have to take. I don't want Liberty going free without knowing that he can catch his own dinner."

"How do you know when a dolphin's ready?"

"They make it clear to those who can understand."

The dolphin exchange lasted for fifteen minutes, until the two dolphins returned to their pod and their world. Her lower lip pushed out as she watched them leave.

"Oh, please come by again and keep Liberty company," she pleaded, her heart in her voice. "He needs you."

He squeezed her shoulder, then leaned closer and pressed his lips against her bare skin. "He'll be all right. I wouldn't let him go if I thought otherwise."

"I know that." She turned to him. "Is that what you

thought about me? That since I would be all right, it was okay to let me go and not write or call?"

"Maybe. I knew it wouldn't be the same, talking to you on the phone, or worse, trying to put a letter together." He looked past her, trailing his finger up and down her arm. "And I did think you'd forget all about us, go on with your life."

She touched his chin, moving his face until he met her gaze. "Did you forget about me that easily, Chris?"

"I kept my focus on Liberty."

She wouldn't let it go. "Is that a yes?"

He should have said yes and left it at that, but he shook his head instead. Damn. Evading he could do, but not lying. "At the park I kept looking up, waiting for you to walk over. And every night, I could still feel you and smell you."

She let out a long breath and leaned forward to kiss him. She had a dreamy look in her eyes, a look that made him wish for more.

"I think I love you, Chris Maddox," she said on a whisper.

He leaned forward, pressing his forehead against hers and letting the words echo in his head. "Don't say that, Lucy."

"Why? Does it scare you?"

"No, it makes me want you more than I already do, more than I should." He looked up, sliding his fingers beneath her chin. "And that's one heartache too many."

"We can keep in touch. I know phone calls and letters aren't the same, but it's something."

"Nope, can't do it. It has to be all or nothing."

She leaned back, a teasing smile on her face. "Why don't you ask me to give it all up and chase dolphin dreams with you?" Beneath that smile, though, he sensed something more serious.

"I can't do that." He had to stop that wishful look in her eyes. What if she said yes, then inevitably became bored and wanted her material world back? She'd already come to mean far too much for him to risk that, for both their sakes.

She looked him full in the face and asked, "Don't you want me?"

He answered her with only a kiss.

14

MAKING LOVE with Chris was as natural to Lucy as if they'd been making love for a lifetime, as if their souls were made for this, but fate had taken them in different directions. She didn't think she loved him; she knew it, with all of her heart, with everything that was inside her. And if loving him would prove the most painful thing in her life, then she'd pay that price to have touched his soul.

The sun had long ago set, taking the hues of gold and leaving behind a moon so bright, it looked like morning had already come. Moonshine washed everything in hues of gray and black, except for the ocean. That it brought to life in a shower of diamonds.

They cuddled on the beach in the shadow of a rock formation. After they had returned to earth, he had spooned her against him. Even though the length of their bodies pressed together, it didn't seem enough for him. His hand skimmed her bare skin, the curve of her hip and the length of her leg. He cherished and revered her with his touch. Never had she been treated that way before. To everyone else in her life, she was the daughter they were proud of, the wife and now ex-wife who didn't put enough into the business, the boss or colleague who commanded respect.

Here on Nassau she was a woman who had found her true self buried deep inside her, a woman who reveled in life and all of the thousand pleasures it could bestow upon her...a woman who loved. But was she a woman willing to give up one life for another?

Above the sound of the waves lapping against the shore, she heard Liberty come to the surface, a distant gust of mist that made her smile. Behind her, she heard Chris's steady breathing, felt his heartbeat and the length of his body against hers.

"Do you think I've changed from the woman who arrived here three weeks ago?" she asked.

"I think I've found a different part of that woman."

She turned slightly. "Are you saying I'm schizophrenic?"

He chuckled. "No. There are just different layers to you. When you left here, you went back to the business layer, didn't you? You became the woman who runs a successful company, who people listen to, who is happy with her life and her apartment and car. When you returned, you became the woman I know."

"And who is she?"

"Didn't I ask *you* that once?"

"Yes, and I answered you." She turned to him. The moonlight cast his features in the bas-relief of a statue. "But who is the Lucy here? To you?"

His fingers trailed across her jawline and over the curves of her face. "Beautiful, compassionate, sexy and perhaps a little more vulnerable than she'd like to be."

"You think I'm vulnerable?" She'd never considered herself that.

"My guess is you've discovered a woman inside you, and you don't know what to do with her. Or what it means to be her."

"You're good. I *am* a different woman here, and I didn't know she existed until I came here the first time.

But you're wrong about one thing. I didn't put her aside when I went home. Yes, she was lost in my other world, because she wanted to feel ocean breezes and watch you work with Liberty, and to be with you." Her eyes widened, because now she knew why she'd felt the desperate urge to return. "And when she started going away, it scared me. I didn't want to lose her."

"So you came back to find her?"

She nodded, feeling a tightness swirling inside her. "And when I go home for good, what will happen to her?"

He took her hand and pressed it to his heart. "She'll be right here."

She closed her eyes at his words, feeling the ache fill her heart, feeling love fill it, too. A rush of warmth and dizziness washed through her. He did care about her, did feel something for her even if he didn't want her in his life permanently. She would keep those words inside her forever, to keep her warm on cold Minnesota nights and through long, hectic days. But she had a feeling those words wouldn't bring her peace. They would torment her and make her question everything she held dear.

CHRIS AND LUCY worked with Liberty that next morning, and he took some pictures of her and the dolphin, to document his progress. She hoped it was to remember her by, but she dared not ask.

A while later a cheery voice called to them from the shore. Ima waved at them, her flowered-print dress flapping in the breeze. They had met the reporter for the *Bahama Journal* last night at Barney's, and Lucy had gotten her interested in interviewing Chris for her magazine.

The rest of the morning they spent with Ima as she took photos of them with Liberty. Then she interviewed

Chris about his organization and his work, and surprisingly, even asked Lucy a few questions.

"This should run in tomorrow's paper if I can get it written in time. Thanks for your time, both of you." She smiled. "You two look like you're into what you're doing. You love your work and it shows."

"Oh, I'm not—" Lucy faltered. "Thanks." She turned to Chris, who smiled in encouragement. "We do love what we're doing."

LATER THAT AFTERNOON they went into town for lunch and then picked up some steaks for dinner. Lucy wandered the aisles of the tiny grocery store, delighting in the brands and foodstuffs unique to the islands.

"How about some Ting?" she asked Chris, holding up a green soda bottle.

"Sure, grab a few."

She wandered to the back of one of the aisles and turned the corner to find herself face-to-face with Crandall. He wore his usual expensive clothing and the debonair exterior she now knew to be phony.

He gave her a smile that reminded her of the shark whose tank she'd knocked him into.

"I see you prefer to shack up with the more primitive sort, Ms. Donovan. No wonder you didn't know what to do when a man proposed *civilized* sex."

Her eyes narrowed, but she kept her voice calm. "The only creature less primitive than you is the jellyfish, but perhaps I'm being unfair. After all, I've never even met a jellyfish."

He smiled, as though she were an amusing child. "You will regret not doing business with me, Ms. Donovan."

"I don't swim with sharks. Although I hear you do." She saw Chris peering around the end of the aisle looking for her. "And not very well, either." She turned to meet him as he made his way toward her. She shook her head slightly, not wanting to cause a fuss or spoil their perfect day.

"Was he bothering you?" Chris asked at the checkout counter.

"Just being his usual gracious self."

CHRIS LET LUCY drive the moped to the park, though his wandering hands made for distracted driving. He tucked them beneath her T-shirt and traced tantalizing lines around the curves of her breasts.

"We're going to crash if you keep doing that," she said, though the threatening tone was sabotaged when her voice crept up in pitch as he cupped her breasts.

"But what a way to go."

The park was fairly deserted. Bill was dusting the Bahamian paraphernalia on the cart behind him. Bailey was pushing a large broom across the white pavement. When he saw them, he leaned it against the fence that kept people away from the empty dolphin pool and sauntered over.

"Hello, Miss Lucy, mister dolphin fish man."

Chris winced at the term, but managed a smile anyway.

"His name is Chris," she corrected.

"And a dolphin is not a fish," Chris said. "It's a dolphin, period."

Bailey smiled. "I know, I know. Miss Lucy, my friend is here right now, the one I told you about. He is walking around the park with big visions in his eyes." Bailey's eyes widened to demonstrate.

She saw a short, dark-skinned man wearing a colorful

frock that hung over black cotton pants. He walked out of the aquarium building, and Bailey waved him over.

David Gevauden's smile was genuine as he extended his hand to Lucy. "It is nice to meet you, Lucy. I didn't know you were returning so soon."

She glanced at Chris. "Me, either, actually."

"And this is your husband?" David asked, shaking Chris's hand.

"A friend."

"He the guy who take the dolphin I was telling you about," Bailey explained.

David nodded. "Oh, yes, the dolphin fish man."

Chris rolled his eyes, but gave up on correcting him.

David looked around. "This is a nice park, but the property is more valuable for use as accommodations. Have you made any decisions on selling it to me as we discussed?"

"My financial advisor is looking over the details now, though at first glance he seemed to think it could work. As long as Bill and Bailey have guarantee of jobs."

"I am pleased to hear that. Yes, of course they will. I would be most interested in acquiring the marine specimens as well. I thought using the ocean life motif would be nice, having aquariums scattered throughout the grounds and in the restaurant. I'm sure we could work something out financially."

"I'll have to think about that."

Chris crossed his arms. "You weren't thinking of having dolphins as part of that motif, were you?"

"No, mon, just the smaller ones." He gestured at the park in general. "What else would you do with all of them if not sell them to me?"

She looked out at the ocean. "Free them?"

David made a deep laughing sound. "When you can

make money from them? Why would you do such a thing?"

"Maybe they deserve to be free."

David's smile was half-teasing. "Maybe you should discuss this with your financial advisor."

"That's a decision I can make without him. I'll think about it. I'm sure we can work something out."

He shook her and Chris's hand again. "I hope so."

"It was nice meeting you. I'll be in touch with you soon." She turned to Bailey. "How's it going?"

He shrugged. "Earlier we had a few groups through, but when the cruise ship left, it got quiet. Everybody want to see the dolphin."

Chris shrugged. "Tell them to watch the educational channel."

Bailey smiled. "Miss Lucy, dat man of yours has a smart mouth. But he ain't a bad guy."

Chris slid his fingers through hers and leaned close to nuzzle her neck. "Gee, honey, we got his approval."

She shivered at his words.

Bailey waved them away. "Ah, go on, mon. You look like you have better t'ings to do den harass me."

THE ARTICLE on Chris came out the following day. As promised, Ima did not reveal where Chris and Lucy were staying, and the pictures could have been of any beach on the island.

Lucy was reading the article aloud from the beach as Chris set fish free for Liberty. "'A creature as intelligent as the dolphin should indeed be left to live its life in the wild. Dolphins have a strong ally in Maddox.' Not bad, eh?"

"One down, millions to go."

"Ah, I've been wondering where the cynic's been hiding," she said, a teasing smile on her face.

He lifted his sunglasses. "I guess I've been too busy enjoying a little of the good to think much of the bad."

She hugged herself at the genuineness of his words, and of the eyes that told her how much he needed that goodness for a while. And while she was with him, she felt worthy of that opinion. Back at home, well, that was another story.

Her mother wouldn't be so pleased if she knew what Lucy was up to here. She would call it a phase. Maybe it was. Maybe coming back was a way of finishing what she felt had only started, a way of living out a fantasy, perhaps. At some point her sensibility would kick in, and she'd embrace her life as always. Well, at least tolerate it as always.

Why did Chris's assurance that her feelings were a phase bother her so much? He was so damned sure. Couldn't he let himself for one moment wonder if she might be persuaded to stay with him?

Her insides felt pulled in a hundred directions. Coming back had complicated things. Being here made her question her life as she'd never done before, made her want things she'd never wanted before.

That morning she'd found her business card lying on the corner of one of Chris's crates. She'd picked it up, fingering the worn corners. He'd been touching it, thinking about her.

All or nothing. His words floated through her mind. He wanted it all, but he'd asked for nothing.

CRANDALL HELD the *Bahama Journal* in his hand, a picture of the tease and the arrogant dolphin man on the front page. She thought she was hot stuff.

He had the phone tucked between his ear and shoulder. The ringing abruptly stopped, and someone answered, "'lo?"

"Mike? This is Crandall."

"Hey, what's up? Did you ever sweet-talk that chick into selling the park to you? I'll bet you had her right in the palm of your hand. Once you start the high-rise, she can't say a thing about that quaint little hotel you said you were building."

"Actually, she's the reason I'm calling you. Didn't you have a friend who caught dolphins and sold them to marine parks?"

"Yeah, Dover Pike, out of Miami. Why?"

"Let's just say I owe my little girlfriend a favor. Take a look at the *Bahama Journal* today. Her friend is that guy who goes around freeing dolphins, and they're about to release another one, the one that used to be at the park. There will even be other dolphins in the area. If, say, Dover were around when the dolphin was released, he could catch it and sell it at a premium. After all, it's already been trained to do tricks."

"Ah, I see. And what do you want from the deal?"

He narrowed his eyes at the picture of Lucy touching the dolphin, a warm smile on her face. "The satisfaction of teaching her a lesson. Let me know what your friend says."

"I'll call him right now."

A few minutes later, Mike called back. "Dover already had a trip planned for this area. He's going to move it up a week and head on down. When do you think they'll release the dolphin?"

"In a few days, according to the article. All Dover has to do is anchor offshore and wait. It's as easy as that, and there's nothing either Lucy or the Maddox guy can do.

According to the article, it is, after all, the chance they take in releasing them. We're going to up the odds, that's all."

He hung up the phone, a slow smile spreading across his face. Nobody messed with Crandall Morton without paying the price.

EVERY MORNING was beautiful and filled with sunshine, and reminded Lucy that the time to leave was coming soon. Ima had stopped by a few days later with some letters in response to her article, and even a couple of checks.

Chris was spending less time with Liberty now, hovering close enough to monitor his eating but not touching him. Chris didn't have to cut the fishes' tails anymore. In fact, Liberty was catching his own fish when schools swam through the nets. Last night she and Chris had cuddled in the hammock and listened to Liberty splash through the water as he chased them. She heard Chris's satisfied sigh, joined by her own. This was his project, but she felt a part of it, a proud parent of sorts.

"He's almost ready, isn't he?" she'd asked. Liberty had stopped eating dead fish altogether, another good sign.

"Almost. He's anxious to get going."

"Is this how long it usually takes?"

"No, sometimes it takes months, even longer than a year. It depends on how they've been trained and how they were treated. Liberty's responded fantastically."

She watched from her usual perch as Chris released five fish at once, giving Liberty practice at selecting his prey from the school. She glanced out at the ocean and saw the sight she'd been waiting for. Getting to her feet, she got Chris's attention and pointed at a pod of dolphins passing outside the reef. Their dorsal fins gracefully broke the surface with a small gust of exhale from their blowholes, then disappeared into the water again. She watched as one of them made its way to Liberty's pen. Sappy romantic that she'd become, she wanted to think it was a female who had fallen in love with Liberty.

Liberty knew she was coming long before he could probably see her, because he swam to the edge of the net nearest her approach. Chris watched from the beach, making a shelf of his hand against the glare of the sun. He was smiling as he made his way to the boardwalk. When he reached where Lucy was, he looked for the rest of the pod, playing several hundred yards away.

"There's a boat out there," Lucy said, spotting the anchored vessel far out in the ocean.

Chris narrowed his eyes. "It almost looks like...nah, can't be. There's probably about twenty dolphin in that pod." He turned back to the two dolphins near them. "The next time they come by, I'm going to let him go."

In those words she could hear anticipation, worry, but total resoluteness.

She inhaled softly. "Really?"

"Yep. I think he'll be ready then. We'll take the boat and follow them for a while."

She found herself smiling at the word *we*. They were a team, sort of. He had included her in his special task. To hear him say it made all the difference. She watched as the lone dolphin made her way back to the pod.

"It's hard to believe Liberty will be out there swimming with other dolphins, never having to do what a human wants again."

Chris had a look of satisfaction on his features as he looked at the pod, too. "It's what they all deserve."

She could see determination, love and a sense of purpose emanating from him. He was born to this. Nothing else in life would be as important to him.

Maybe if she was a different person, she could make him love her as much as his work. If only she was *this* Lucy, and not the one who thrived on success and confirmation.

THE WAY THE SCHEDULE was shaping up, Liberty would be released Saturday, and Lucy would fly home Sunday. Chris was happy about the first and wasn't letting himself think about the second. He should have been pounding it into his head day and night, instead he pulled her closer and relished her warmth even in the hot, muggy night. He wasn't the type to lie awake through the night and think about things, but he was doing exactly that.

He could feel the bracelet between his and Lucy's skin, though not even that reminder had kept his heart from absorbing her. Forget that, he told himself, even as his arms involuntarily squeezed her tighter. Her breathing was light and steady, held in dreams rather than tormenting thoughts. She did not belong in his world, even if she said things that indicated she wanted to think she did. So had that college student—whatever her name was—and then she'd gotten bored and gone off to better things. He'd missed the student, but Lucy would rip his heart out when she left him for things he couldn't give her.

He couldn't tell her that, because saying it aloud would make it that much more real and painful. He had to send her home and know she was never coming back.

"Lucy, Lucy, Lucy," he whispered. "What have you done to me?"

SATURDAY DAWNED as bright and beautiful as the rest of the mornings, yet Lucy felt as cloudy inside as a wintry

St. Paul day. It was almost over. Today Liberty would go free, and tomorrow so would she.

Chris was already out with Liberty, making sure he left with a full stomach that he had filled himself. As she stood in the doorway watching him, a veil of frustration dropped over her. Why fall in love with him? Why not that accountant she'd gone out with? No, she had to go and fall for a man who chased dolphin dreams.

She'd lain awake for hours in the night, imagining packing up her office and bidding everyone a farewell as she left for the Keys. Her mother called the men in the white coats and they'd captured her before she'd even gotten out of the building.

Then she'd heard Chris's words: What have you done to me? She closed her eyes, feeling more pain than she'd ever felt before. He did care. Maybe she hadn't misread all those subtle ways he had of letting her know.

She leaned her cheek against the doorway, feeling the breeze wash over her face. "Oh, Chris, what have you done to *me?*"

He pulled the fish cage out of the water, but Liberty was too busy catching fish to notice. Now it was a matter of waiting for the pod.

He carried the wire cage up to the boathouse and set it on the deck. He tossed her an orange fruit. "Breakfast."

She looked at it, turning the smooth-skinned fruit over in her hands. "What is it?"

"Mango."

She started to take a bite when he laughed. "You have to peel it first." He walked closer and started the peel for her, then handed the fruit back to her.

Just as the juice dripped over her fingers, she caught

Chris watching behind her. His green eyes lit up. "They're here."

She turned to see the visual chorus of fins glide by. One fin made its way to Liberty, who was already waiting by the edge of the net.

"Oooh," she breathed out, happy and sad and nervous at the same time. Tightness was spreading over her chest.

Chris slid into the water and swam over. Maybe Liberty told the other dolphin that Chris wasn't a threat, because she didn't take off. Lucy watched as Chris detached the net from the floats, letting the net drop and pushing the floats in a wide arc.

He swam back, climbing up next to Lucy and watching with every muscle tensed. The two dolphins stayed in their normal positions at first, rising to the surface to take a breath simultaneously. Then Liberty swam tentatively beyond the old barrier. The female dolphin swam in a small circle, waiting for him to gain his bearings.

Lucy reached down and put her hand over Chris's wet, cool one. He twined his fingers with hers, but neither took their gaze from the dolphins. She kept holding her breath, waiting. The female dolphin swam a little farther away, and Liberty followed. They paused to touch snouts, and then she pressed up against his side. And off they went toward open water and the waiting pod.

Then everything went blurry because Lucy's eyes filled with tears. Her heart was about to burst, and she squeezed Chris's hand tighter. When she looked at him, his expression was still, but she saw a light in his eyes. He walked into the boathouse and emerged with a pair of binoculars. He watched as Liberty merged with the pod. For a few minutes, she couldn't tell which dolphin was Liberty, but then she saw the triangle and smiled—he was in the middle of the pod, not an outcast.

When the pod began to move slowly away, Chris pulled her toward the boat on the other side. He started it up and slowly moved out of the lagoon and through the opening in the reef they'd swam through before.

The pod started moving faster, probably alarmed at the sound of the engine. But the boat that had been anchored in the distance for the past few days was moving closer, too.

"Hand me the binoculars," he said, reaching out as she put them in his palm. "Damn it, I don't believe this."

"What's wrong?"

"I know that boat. I was on it a few times when I helped Aquatic Wonders catch dolphins. It's called the *Captivator*. They're still using it to catch dolphins." His tone dropped to an ominous low. "And they're after Liberty."

15

LUCY'S HEART DROPPED as she followed Chris's eyes to the boat. "How can you tell that? Why would they single out Liberty?"

He handed her the glasses and turned toward the other boat. "Because our friend Crandall is on board. He must have told Dover I was releasing a trained dolphin. And the article showed a picture of the brand."

"*Crandall's on board?*" She could barely discern the man's figure as he leaned near the edge and pointed at them. "Oh, my God. He must have read the article. He said I'd regret messing with him."

Chris turned to her. "He threatened you? Why didn't you tell me?"

"I didn't take it as a threat. I figured he was spouting empty words!"

The pod was making headway, but the *Captivator* was aiming to cut them off. Their nets were at the ready, and one man was pointing at Liberty. She was trying to take it all in, the bundle of nets by the stern, the small boat revving its engine nearby.

"What are they going to do?"

"Well, if they're still doing it the same way, the guy in the small boat will set the net once the dolphins ride the bow wake, which they love to do. The *Captivator* will start to circle toward the small boat, which will take the net and make a circle, trapping the dolphins on the right side."

"Not if I can help it." She crawled up to the front bow, holding onto the railing.

"What are you doing?" he called over the wind.

"I don't know, but I have to do something."

"Lucy, get back here. I don't want you getting hurt."

She climbed farther out, bracing herself on knees that were getting banged up by the choppy water. "This is my fault, and I'm not going to let them take Liberty! Keep going, I'll be fine."

The poor dolphins had no idea what they were in for as they rode the *Captivator's* wake, just like Chris said. The dolphins that weren't riding the wake were split by the boat, and any on the other side would be caught in the net, too. Her heart was pounding louder than the wind that roared in her ears. As Chris came up behind those dolphins, they shot forward and to the left, well out of the net's range.

She looked back at Chris, who was searching for the triangle brand among that group. He met her eyes and shook his head. Liberty was on the other side of the boat.

The men on the larger boat were yelling as Chris took his smaller, faster boat up ahead and circled back around. She wished looks could kill as she shot Crandall a hateful look before focusing again on the dolphins.

The man in the small boat released the net as the *Captivator* circled around. There was still a little gap, but the dolphins were swimming in confusion and didn't see the opening.

"No!" she screamed out when she saw the six dolphins, including Liberty, doomed to a life of captivity.

"Hey, you!" a brusque man yelled out. "Get away from here!"

"Sorry, Dover, but you're not getting these," Chris yelled back.

Lucy saw that the rest of the pod was waiting to see how their friends were faring. She saw the six dolphins in panicked disarray, pushing up against the nets, then returning to the center to huddle with the others.

"I told you not to mess with me, Lucy Donovan!" Crandall's voice called out above the melee.

"All this because I didn't want to sleep with you? You're disgusting!"

And then she jumped into the deep blue water. She heard Chris yell out her name before she hit the water, but she didn't have time for any more words. She found the edge of the net just as Liberty raised his head out of the water.

"This is for you, Liberty. For all of you." She pushed down on the edge of the net, fighting against the buoyancy of the cork until the net collapsed.

Chris jumped in and swam right into the dolphins, pushing them toward the opening. Some brushed by her on their way to freedom. Her breath came in gasps as she watched them join their friends and race off into the open water.

"What are you doing, Maddox, sabotaging captures now? I thought you did these release things by the book."

Lucy looked up to see the gruff, stocky man with meaty fists on his waist.

"And what are you doing, Dover, sabotaging releases? Even that's beneath your low standards. I'm not letting you recapture my dolphin."

"You're not going to get away with this, Maddox."

"You draw up the papers, and I'll see you in court. We'll see what the judge has to say."

Dover made a snorting sound before shifting his gaze to her. "What, now you have a partner in crime?"

She couldn't help smiling at the phrase, no matter how gruffly the question was posed. "Yeah, he's got a partner. Mess with him, and you mess with me."

Chris swam over to her and gave Dover a wink. "She's tougher than she looks."

As they swam back to their boat, she could hear Dover saying, "What's this about her not sleeping with you, Morton?"

Chris pulled himself up on the boat and lent her a hand. He started the engine and followed the pod of dolphins moving rapidly away from their thwarted capture. Chris stayed a distance behind them, and she stood beside him at the helm. When they were out of sight altogether, he turned back.

He pulled her close. "You are incredible, you know that?"

"I did what I had to do," she said with a smile. "Partner."

His arms embraced her, and he rested his chin atop her head. She felt his mouth against the top of her head, kissing softly. After a moment, he pulled back and looked down at her.

"Lucy, I..." His eyes searched hers for a moment as she waited breathlessly for his next words. He leaned down and kissed her deeply, and she had no doubt that he loved her in some way.

He finished the kiss, glancing back at the capture boat to make sure they were still stationary. They were wrestling with their nets.

"They're safe for now. If I ever find out Liberty's been captured again, I'll do whatever I have to do to free him.

Even if it's not by the books." He touched her nose. "Maybe I'll even call you."

She grinned. "We were good together, weren't we?"

"The best." His thumbs were grazing those places to the sides of her mouth where those illusive dimples appeared only for him. "Let's go back and celebrate."

"LUCY, PLEASE DON'T CRY."

She wiped her eyes, but more tears came as she looked at the empty lagoon. "They're happy tears."

"You don't look happy."

"I didn't think it would hurt this much to lose him. I mean, I knew all along that he would leave. It feels good to know he's free, but it's sad, too."

"I know," he said, holding her close and stroking her hair.

She turned to him. "How can you do this over and over again? How can you come to care about them—and I know you do care about them—and let them go?"

He looked into her eyes. "I always tell myself that I won't get attached to them, because letting them go is what I'm all about. As I work with them, I keep in mind that they're going to leave someday."

"So you don't feel sad at all?"

He remained quiet for a moment, and when he spoke his voice was low and quiet. "I do feel sad. Not with all of them, because some I'm glad to see go. But there are a few like Liberty who are special. And when they go free, I'm happy and sad at the same time." He smiled faintly. "I've never admitted that to anyone before. Maybe not even myself."

She tightened her hold around his waist. "It is sort of a conflict, isn't it? Wanting them to go free, but wishing they were still around."

"I love being with the dolphins, love the interaction and the trust between us. But I know they belong in their world and I belong in mine, and so for however brief our time is together that our worlds touch, I must always let them go. If there was some way I could keep them without violating the very thing I fight for, I would. They can't travel with me, and I can't stay in their world, either. It always has to come down to that, letting go forever."

She swallowed hard, because she had lost sight of the fact that he was talking about dolphins and not her. Their worlds were different, too. He would suffocate in her world; she would drown in his.

She took a deep breath, but it did nothing to relieve the pain that she felt. "Take me to the park," she said, instead of the thousand other things she wanted to say.

If he questioned her thought process, he didn't vocalize it. He simply led the way down the boardwalk to the moped.

She held on tighter than usual as they sped to the park. He smelled of salt and spice and male. She inhaled it, wanting to capture it somehow and remember it for always. But she couldn't bottle Chris, or capture him in any way. Like Liberty, he was a free spirit.

They pulled into the park and found a few families wandering around inside. Bailey had taken down the dolphin banner at Lucy's request.

Chris glanced over at the pool Liberty had once been a prisoner in, and she saw the faint gleam in his eyes as his gaze moved on to the open ocean beyond. He followed her to the aquarium house where Bailey was busy telling another high-seas tale of adventure.

"It was called a parchment worm, about dis long," he indicated a foot or so with his hands. "It had a mout' dat came out of its mout' wit' little pincers to hold the food, and another mout' dat came out to eat it. Wicked t'ing, mon. Dat's probably where dey get ideas for alien movies, you t'ink?''

"Bailey," she said, lowering her chin.

"Miss Lucy!" he said, his eyes wide as he came over to her. "But I swear it's true! Sonny buy the creature from some fisherman a year before, but it died."

"Okay, okay. Can I see you for a moment?"

"Since the dolphin fish go away, I got to enhance what is here." He gestured with his hands. "I even got to talk about t'ings we used to have."

"Well, you won't have to do that anymore. We're going to close the park today. Give whoever's here refunds and politely escort them out. Use any reason you deem...believable."

Bailey looked at Chris for confirmation of this madness. He merely shrugged. "She's the boss."

"We're freeing all of the creatures in the park. Today, now. According to their files, they're all indigenous, so they should survive." She turned to Chris. "I don't suppose there are any groups who repatriate sharks or stingrays, are there?"

"Er, I don't think so," Chris answered. "But they should be fine."

"Miss Lucy," Bailey said in a low voice. "Did you get into some of the island happy juice?"

"No! I've just come to—" she glanced at Chris "—an understanding about these creatures. They don't belong in glass tanks where people can gawk at them. In fact, I'm going to make a deal with your friend, David. I'll finance the park here on two conditions. One is that he offer glass-bottom boat tours so that people can see these creatures undisturbed in their own environment. And two, that he keep a small portion of the inlet over there so that if the Free Dolphin Society ever needs a place to work with a captive dolphin, they can do it here. Forever. Well?'' she said to Bailey as he stood there with his mouth open. ''What are you waiting for? Shoo! Escort, escort, escort. And then we'll put you to work. Don't worry about your severance pay. I'll pay you and Bill until your friend gets this place reopened.''

''T'ank you, Miss Lucy. You are so very kind.''

She turned to Chris, who had the same kind of shell-shocked look on his face.

''You've created a monster,'' she said with a grin.

''I see that.'' He leaned forward and kissed her. ''But I like her...so very much.''

And then they went to work catching, carrying and releasing until every creature was back in its natural home in the ocean. As soon as they hit the water, they crawled, swam or ran off to hide among the reefs, needing no prodding or guidance. The predators were too shocked by the journey from their tanks to go after the prey. Even the lethargic shark came quickly to life when it hit the water.

It was almost evening by the time they were through, setting the last moray eel free beneath the gilded wavelets. Chris came up behind her as she watched it swim away, slipping his arms around her and resting his chin on her shoulder.

She took a deep, satisfied breath. ''They're all free.''

''Yep. Every last one of them.''

''It didn't hurt the way letting Liberty go did.''

''You didn't get attached to them.''

''Some of them would be a little hard to get attached to.''

Bailey walked up beside them. ''Except for dat lobster.

I could definitely get attached to him." He rubbed his belly, but his smile disappeared at Lucy's chagrined look. "Only kidding."

"Come on, Bailey. Let me write you and Bill a check so you can go home to all those lovely children of yours."

Once Bill had left, Bailey remained. He dropped his head, looking up at her. "Miss Lucy, I have a confession to make."

She tried to look serious. "What could you possibly have to confess?"

"I don' have no childrens. I just didn't want you to send me off when you first got here."

"No! Bailey, I can't believe it. And here all this time I thought...." She couldn't help the smile. "When the number of children and goats kept changing, I kind of wondered."

He gave her a sheepish smile. "I'm jus' no good at lying, I guess."

"I don't know about that. You put on quite a few shows out there." She nodded toward the aquariums. "Try to clean up your act, okay?"

"Yes, ma'am."

They exchanged a smile. "Thanks for all your help."

"So, are you leaving for good dis time?"

She took a deep breath. "Yes, this time I go for good. Back to the real world, as it were."

"You seem happy here." He followed her gaze to Chris, who was watching for dolphin fins, no doubt.

"I am. But I don't belong here."

Bailey folded his check and put it in his pocket without even looking at it. He touched his hand to his heart. "You belong where your heart is, Miss Lucy. Dat's all dat matter."

16

THE CARIBE PLANTATION seemed almost like home to her now. Its welcoming lights and foliage greeted her when they returned that evening. She couldn't imagine having stayed in the mansion itself, where once she would have been much more comfortable. The boathouse with its hammock and sounds of the open sea were part of her now.

Her gaze went right to the pen, where the floats formed a misshapen half circle. The moon was still bright, shimmering on the water in a dazzling display. The air was clear, unlike the city, holding the aroma of flowers and barbecue smoke.

"Sure you don't want to talk about it?" he asked as they headed up the boardwalk.

"You know what I want to do? I want to just sit here and look at you."

He lifted an eyebrow, but his expression was one of pleasant surprise. "You'll be bored in thirty seconds."

"No, I won't."

They reached the deck that circled their half of the boathouse. He walked inside long enough to take down the hammock and lay it on the deck. She wanted to sit so that he would be in the full moonlight, but the moon was directly overhead. It cast its silvery light down over them, over their hands as they linked the moment they sat down.

No words. What good did they do anyway? He cared about her. She loved him. It got them nowhere.

She pushed all words from her mind, concentrating on Chris, on the curves of his face, the way his curls moved in the breeze, the shape of his mouth. He still wore his white, cotton shirt, unbuttoned to show a slice of tanned skin. They sat cross-legged, knees touching. Heat flared up where their palms pressed together, where the moisture sealed them.

She could feel that touch rise up her arms, a tingling heat that crept through her body like the burning fuse of a firecracker. She let desire twine through her body and curl between her legs. Her fingers tightened on his, and he mirrored the movement. Their expressions remained passive, or at least she hoped hers didn't show the pain, the desire or the love flowing through her.

It amazed her how simple this was, sitting here, not saying anything. How simple, yet profound. She wanted to believe that he had shared more with her than with those other women.

His fingers tightened again, as if in answer to her doubts. Had he seen the question in her eyes? *God, she loved this man.* The words echoed through her body, constricting her chest, and coiling through her limbs. How was she supposed to let him go? How could she walk away and be content to go on with her life as though he'd never touched it?

He closed his eyes, and his breathing became even. Just when she wondered if he'd fallen asleep, his breath hitched.

"Wicked man," she whispered, running her finger across the chin that looked strong yet hinted at vulnerability.

He opened his eyes, and she felt the impact of that gaze

right to the pit of her stomach. The pain of goodbye in her heart was mirrored in those eyes. Her hand trailed from his cheek to the curve of his mouth as she remembered their kisses. He pressed her palm to his mouth, tickling her sensitive skin with his tongue. She ran her fingers down the column of his neck to his bare chest and over his firm stomach. She had loved this body, had touched everywhere, and would remember the smell and taste of him forever. Not a fling, this. She knew in her heart this was more than that, for both of them.

He knelt over her, allowing her to reach up and touch him as he loosened her top and slid it over her head. He ran his hands down her face, through her hair. She would have closed her eyes in pleasure, but she didn't want to take her eyes off him. He looked ethereal in the moonlight, the dolphin that came out of the sea to become a man during the full moon.

His hands skimmed over her breasts. He touched her sides, following the line of her waist and hips, sliding her shorts down in one smooth movement. His shorts were next to go, and she realized how comfortable she was being naked with him. Even that first night they'd spent in the hammock, there was nothing self-conscious it.

He raised one of her legs and ran his fingers down it, kissing the sensitive skin behind her knee. If she had felt numb earlier, she felt alive now. Alive and pulsing and hungry. She wanted to savor every moment, to make it last until morning when she had to pack and leave. She pushed the thought from her mind just as his finger slid over her most feminine part, making her suck in a breath.

He kissed and nibbled down her thigh, across her hair and over her stomach as he pleasured her until she went over the edge on a breathless gasp. Her fingers twirled through his curls as her body shuddered and tensed in

one long jolt. And then the sensations started all over
again as he circled her breasts with his tongue. Feather
light touches pushed her to another edge, and then over
again.

Her head rocked back as he kissed the hollow of her
throat and then up until she captured his mouth and
kissed him crazily. She wanted to give back the pulsing
hot pleasure he'd given her, and as her tongue stroked
his so did her fingers stroke him. He let out a growling
noise that echoed in their joined mouths, and she smiled
at success.

Then he made love with her in the deepest way possible. He slid in easily, filling her, possessing her. Her fingers tightened over his back as those wicked sensation
started again, rising from a high peak and taking her
even higher. In that cool, balmy night everything exploded inside her, and she clung to him the way she
wanted to cling to his heart and soul. He held her just a
tightly, telling her without words that he didn't want to
let her go, either.

When their breathing stilled, they stretched out beside
each other washed in a glow more magical than moon
light. No words. She loved that about making love with
him. They didn't need words. Their bodies knew instinc-
tively what the other needed, wanted. They moved in
synchronous rhythm the way waves washed in and out
of the lagoon.

He reached out and touched her cheek. His mouth
opened slightly, though no sound emerged. He closed
his eyes and pulled her closer until their bodies melded.
She felt safe and content in his arms. If only she could
stay awake until morning so she could relish the feel of

his body, of every hair and bone that she felt pressed
against her bare skin.

What have you done to me? Whatever it was, she knew
the damage was irreparable.

LUCY THOUGHT she was dreaming about Liberty. She
could hear his playful whistle, hear him splash beneath
her. Chris sat up, rubbing her leg in a subconscious way.
She sat up, too, and followed the noise that was no longer
in her dream.

"Liberty!" She scrambled to her knees and leaned
through the railing.

Liberty bobbed his head, and she knew his smile was
true now. His mate was a distance away, waiting for him.

Chris slid into his shorts and climbed through the railing to drop into the water. Lucy went into the boathouse
to put on her bathing suit and followed. Liberty jumped
out of the water in a graceful arc, but never looked at
Chris for a reward. Chris checked him over for any abra-
sions. Lucy put her palm out, and Liberty touched a
snout unmarred by bruises to it.

"Oh, look at him," she breathed.

Chris's satisfaction was written across his face. "He's
doing great." He looked at the fin in the distance. "She's
probably telling him to get a move on."

Her face brightened. "Do you think it's a she?"

"I know it. And we'd better let him go to it."

She nodded, turning to climb back on the deck. When
she turned back, Liberty was watching them.

"Thanks for coming by and letting us know how
things are going," Chris said. His expression softened as
he looked at the dolphin for a moment. "Bye, Liberty."

He walked away from the railing, and Lucy followed,
trying hard not to turn back to see if he was still there.
She knew he was, though, because she could hear him

moving in the water. Chris walked into the boathouse
and peered around the corner of the window. Liberty
was looking for them, and Lucy's heart nearly broke. She
started to say something, but he pressed his finger over
her lips.

Those lips were stretched into a frown as she watched
Liberty. The dolphin remained for several agonizing
minutes, calling to them with his whistles, tilting his
head. Her fingers curled around the window's edge so
tight they hurt. *So unfair, so unfair*, the words chanted
through her mind as she tried to blink away the tears. Finally Liberty turned around and headed back to his partner.

"I don't want him returning when I'm gone. If the people who stay here feed him, it could set back Liberty's untraining."

She sighed, her insides a knot. "I know, but he was so
cute. And so sad, looking for us when we walked away."

"Call it tough love."

She met his gaze and had the feeling he was talking
about more than the dolphin. "It is tough." She pulled
her gaze away, looking out the window as the two fins
joined a few more farther out. "It's so hard letting go."

"Yes, it is." He touched her cheek, then turned to get
towels.

"He must have asked the pod to pause so he could stop
in and say hi." Her frown returned full force. "And we
walked away from him."

"It's for his own good. You remember that clean-break
theory, don't you?"

She kept her gaze at the water. "Yes, I know all about
it. It's a good theory, but it hurts like hell." She turned to
him. "You're going to do the same thing to me, aren't
you? You're going to ignore my letters, never call an

convince yourself it's for my own good.'' When he didn't answer, she said in a low voice, ''Aren't you?''

''Remember when I said all or nothing?''

''But you never asked me for all.''

His expression was somber. ''Because that woman inside you who loves the city and money and material comforts would never be happy with me.'' He looked out over the water, his voice so low she could barely hear it. ''When I work with dolphins, I know in advance that they have to go. If you decided to give everything up to be with me, I'd take that as a forever thing. A commitment to the dolphins and me. Watching you walk away would kill me ten times as much as watching Liberty leave.''

''So it's not only me you're protecting....'' She let the sentence die when he shook his head. She wanted to hit him, but her frustration lay in herself, not in him. Because he did have her thinking about forever. She would be the one giving up her life as she knew it, because she would never ask Chris to do the same.

AS THE TIME TO LEAVE loomed ahead, Lucy became almost anxious to get the pain over with. They both showered and dressed, she packed, and they headed into town for lunch. The banana he had fed her earlier sat in her stomach like a lump, and the shrimp on her plate looked as appetizing as some of the other creatures she'd seen beneath the water.

''Eat,'' he ordered.

''Are you treating me like one of your dolphins?''

''Are you going to toss a ball to me with your snout?''

She couldn't even muster a smile, but dropped her gaze to the shrimp and spicy rice on her plate. He hadn't eaten much of his sandwich, either, though she didn't know if it was for the same reason.

"There's a guy who gives helicopter tours for the tourists," he said after a few minutes of silence. "He's going to take me up a few times to check on Liberty before I leave."

"Are you trying to make me feel better or worse?"

He shrugged. "Just talking."

"Since when do you talk so much?"

He tilted his head. "Since you look so down."

"I don't want to hear about you going up in a helicopter or seeing Liberty or anything." She shoved away her plate and met his gaze. "Unless you write me about it. Or call me."

He didn't answer. All or nothing. *Ask me for all!* She wanted to hear the words, yet the prospect of giving up everything in her life scared her to death.

"I'm ready to go." She stood, feeling restless and frustrated and bad that she was acting so petty.

"But we've got two hours before your flight."

"I just want to check in and get it over with."

They hailed another cab to the airport, the place she'd been dreading ever since she arrived a week ago. After her luggage was checked in, she turned to him.

"I don't want you to wait with me."

He raised his eyebrows. "Are you sure?"

She felt as lousy as she did when she'd turned her back on Liberty. "Yes," she forced out. "Clean break and all," she added, not meeting his gaze.

"Not completely."

She looked up to see him handing her a business card She blinked hard, trying not to let the damned tears come.

"Thanks," she whispered, her throat already thick with them. *Christopher Maddox.*

"Bye, Miz Lucy."

He hugged her, which loosened a few tears on his unsuspecting cheek. He kissed hers away before touching his lips to hers in a gentle goodbye kiss. She wanted to fling herself against him and hold on like a drowning victim, but she maintained her self-control and moved back.

"Goodbye," she said in that thick voice.

He turned and walked away, like he had with Liberty. She knew it hadn't been easy for him that morning. Was it any harder now? No, she would not let herself think about it.

She took a deep breath. It was over. For good this time. No running back, no visits. This hurt too much. Hurt? It ripped her guts out. She sat down, her gaze dropping to the card in her hand, already worn down the way he'd worn hers down. She tucked it in her purse with trembling fingers.

17

BACK IN HER WORLD, Lucy felt the way Chris had once described a captive dolphin: a nobody who belonged neither in the human world nor the dolphin world. Tropical music flowed from her stereo as she looked out at glass-and-steel buildings outside her windows.

People looked at her as though she were different, treating her as someone with a terminal illness. They talked quietly around her, weighing what they said. She had no connection with anyone there, and she had no connection with anyone in Nassau, either. No more park, so no Bailey to call for updates. No phone at the boathouse, even if Chris were still there. It had been three weeks since she'd left, and there was a good chance he was home now for however a brief time. She pulled out his card and rubbed the laminated surface, something she'd had done when she realized how often she would take it out and touch it. It felt warm beneath her touch.

Every night, alone on her bed, she would take her father's dog-eared maps and spread them out on her bed. He had penciled notes here and there, and she once again imagined that romantic wandering life she always thought he'd led. How much of his blood flowed through her veins? Deep inside she longed for that kind of adventure, but her conditioning for stability and success was so strong, she'd never even felt it before. Before Chris came along and turned her world upside down.

She shook her head, forcing herself back to the present and to her drawing board. A proposal for a men's underwear ad had turned into dolphins in a business card layout for the Free Dolphin Society. By the afternoon, she had a whole kit prepared: a brochure, new card and a letter to new members.

She shook her head. "Lucy, you've really lost it."

"What the devil are you working on?"

She jerked around to find Tom staring at her board.

"What are you doing, sneaking up on me like that?" Her face was flushed hot and red.

"I knocked, but you were apparently in the clouds." He glanced disdainfully at the dolphin layout, which looked pretty good if she didn't say so herself. He flicked his hair out of his face. "Luce, we need to talk."

She turned her chair around and leaned against the board. "You've got my attention."

His tone softened. "People are talking. You walk around like you're lost. You haven't gotten a new account since you came back." He picked up the underwear ad ideas that had slipped to the floor, a brief covered with tiny dolphins. "This is garbage. You're working for a client we don't even have." He started to pick up the dolphin ad, but she snatched it back and set it on her board. "You look like a zombie. Even your mother is worried—"

"You spoke to my mother about me?"

"I thought she could shed some light on the situation. Apparently she's as baffled as I am. You're not acting like yourself."

"And who is it that I'm supposed to be acting like, hmm?"

His eyes widened, and he took a step back. "Luce, you need help." He said it slowly, softly, so as not to upset her. "Maybe I pushed you a little hard. Maybe the divorce was too much to handle. Either way, I feel responsible and I want to make things the way they were."

She crossed her arms in front of her. "You want to know what's wrong with me?"

"Yes, yes I do."

"I don't know who Lucy is. That's why I can't be her anymore."

He rubbed his jaw. "Did you experience an alien abduction? A possession?"

"More like the latter, I think."

"It's this dolphin guy, isn't it? You had a fling and now you can't get over him, is that it? Luce, we're still friends. If you need some...companionship, I'd be glad to help."

She held back a bark of laughter. "You think I've lost myself because I'm horny?"

"I don't know. Obviously it's a woman thing. I admit, though, that I get a little...distracted when it's been a while."

"Forget it. I'm not interested."

His lower lip puckered out. "Are you in love with this guy or something?"

She knew it sounded silly, but the word "Yes" came out of its own accord. "And I know it wouldn't work out because we live different lives at different standards, so don't go lecturing me. But you know what, Tom? I keep looking around and asking myself what I'm doing it all for? To have the nice apartment? The Beemer? The fancy watches, clothing, five-star dinners? Do you ever ask yourself what it's really about?" She gestured toward his new Rolex watch glittering in the overhead lights. "Does this make you happy?" Her fist went to her heart. "Really happy, satisfied and content deep inside?"

He frowned again, looking hard at the watch. "Yes, it does."

"It's the Great Green Lie, Tom. All of it. You get satisfaction coming in here and showing it off to me, maybe. You're happy when you're rubbing my nose in your success. But if you take away all this, the clothes, the car, the office...take it all away, and what do you have? Tell me who Tom is."

"You have gone mad, haven't you?"

"Just answer me."

"I'm pres—" He shook his head. "I...well, I have— Luce, this is ridiculous!"

"I couldn't answer that question, either." Her voice softened. "And you know what? It scared me. Lucy Donovan was a title and a list of traits you'd find in a business article. But I found who I was down in Nassau, with Chris and the dolphins. And now I'm afraid to give this up. And why? Because I'm worried what people will think of me. What you and Mother and my stepfather will think. Lucy's lost her mind, that's what they'll think.

"I go home every night, alone, and look at everything I've accumulated in my life. I asked myself how I would feel if one day I came home and it was all gone. You know what? It didn't hurt the way I thought it would. If I imagined the business going under and losing everything, I didn't feel the panic that you obviously feel at that thought."

His eyes had widened and his hand had gone defensively to his chest. "Luce, that's horrible."

"Look at you. You would be devastated, because this is your life, who you are. It doesn't feel that way to me anymore. Maybe it never did. I've been looking at my life, and I probably look like a zombie because I spend all night doing it. I've picked apart my life, and myself, and

I can't find my dreams anywhere. I found your dreams, Mother's, Father's. Lucy didn't have any dreams, because Lucy never existed. She was a combination of everyone's expectations." She picked up the poster. "This is my dream. This is who I am, what I want."

"Underwear?"

She looked at the poster of the dolphin underwear she was holding and flung it away. "Chris is the man I want to be with, no matter that he isn't what everyone else wants me to have. I have never known the happiness I knew when I was with him."

She took a deep breath as the truth settled inside her. Oh, my, what was she saying? Her heart had made decisions without consulting her. Again.

Tom stood there for a few minutes, letting her words sink in. "I never knew you felt this way. Did you feel this way when we were married?"

"I never allowed myself to think of what I wanted, Tom. I let myself be molded and guided until I didn't know who I was anymore."

"So...this guy...does he want to marry you and take you away to save dolphins with him?"

She forced in a breath, looking away from Tom. "I don't know."

"You're ready to throw all this away and you don't even know if the guy wants you?"

Her eyes felt hot and moist, her face flushed. Why was she telling him all this?

A knock sounded on the door, and her secretary popped her head inside. "I have an overnight package for you." Lucy started to toss it on her desk when her secretary added, "It's from Key Largo."

Her fingers tightened on the cardboard just as she was

about to let it go. "Thank you, Edie," Lucy managed before she closed the door.

"From him, I presume?" Tom said.

She ripped open the string and pulled out a packet. A huge smile lit her face when she saw pictures of her and Chris feeding Liberty, of Liberty with his head popped out of the water smiling for the camera, and of Lucy by herself waist-deep in crystal water.

"Look at you." He was peering over her shoulder. "Luce, you look...beautiful."

She turned to him. "I have dimples. Did you know that? Did you ever see dimples on my face?"

"No, but you have them now. Maybe I just missed them."

"So did I, until I met Chris." She pulled out the disappointingly short note.

Miss Lucy,
Ima sent these pictures, so I asked for another set to send to you. I also sent you a set of the ones I took. Now you'll have proof of those dimples. I'm back at home for now, though it looks like I'll be off to a park in Hawaii soon to check out two dolphins being held at a hotel lagoon. Liberty's doing great. I'm taking a flight down there this weekend to take the chopper up and find him. I'll give him your regards.
Miss you,

Chris

She sucked in a long breath, holding the note to her heart. He'd written! He missed her. And he wasn't cutting her off.

"*Miss* Lucy?" Tom said, intruding on her thoughts.

"That's what he called me—Miz Lucy, actually. It started as a joke and turned into something else."

"I've never seen you like this." He glanced at the pictures. "Or like that."

"Now you know what I'm talking about. Have *you* ever looked that happy?"

"Probably. I'm sure I have, sometime or another."

"That's what I thought, too." She walked over to her desk and grabbed her purse. "I've got to get out of here for a while. I won't be able to work now."

He glanced at the dolphin poster. "Like you were before?"

She shot him a look. "Give me time to figure out what I want."

"What about what he wants?"

"I need to figure that out, too."

And she walked out, overnight package clutched in her hand, dimples on her cheeks.

LUCY'S STEP had not been as light in years, or so the past three weeks had felt like. The cool air made her think of balmy breezes and warm sunshine. And now he was going to Hawaii. But he'd broken his rule about clean breaks. What did it mean?

Sitting on a park bench, she reread the letter seven more times, looking for anything that might indicate he wanted her with him. He missed her, she had proof of that in writing. But he'd not asked her to join him down in Nassau. She had already returned to him once, chancing heartbreak and rejection. But that was temporary, and they both had known it. But this time....

His words echoed through her mind, when she'd cried over Liberty's release. *I always tell myself that I won't get attached to them, because letting them go is what I'm all about....*

*I keep in mind that they're going to leave someday.... I know
they belong in their world and I belong in mine, and so for however brief our time is together that our worlds touch, I must always let them go. If there was some way I could keep them
without violating the very thing I fight for, I would. They can't
travel with me, and I can't stay in their world, either. It always
has to come down to that, letting go forever.*

She put her hand to her heart. He hadn't only been
talking about the dolphins. He'd been talking about her,
too. He had been willing to let her go because, like the
dolphins, he knew that she belonged in her world and
could not survive in his. Maybe he'd been wrong.

She looked back at the sleek building Advertising Genius was in. If she gave it all up today, would she miss it?
Would she regret it?

She glanced back at the pictures. No, she would not.
That's what she missed, what she regretted leaving behind. She walked over to a hot dog vendor's cart and bor-
rowed a napkin.

Chris,
Thank you for the pictures. They came at the perfect
time, because I'd almost forgotten about that girl
with the dimples. Right now I feel rather lost, maybe
like Liberty felt when he lived in the pool and wasn't
quite a dolphin nor a human.

The pain is not going away, nor is the loneliness. I
keep asking myself the question, could we make it
work somehow? I know you work alone, but maybe
I could be a partner, doing the PR end of things. All
I know is, I can't stop thinking about you and wanting to be with you, and everything I used to think
was important doesn't compare to being with you
and working to free the dolphins.

You were wrong when you said my experience with you would touch me but wouldn't change my life. And really wrong when you said I'd find happiness in my own sphere. I found it in your sphere.

You probably think I'm chicken, writing instead of calling or showing up. You're right. I feel so lost, I couldn't handle a live rejection. If you never wanted me in your life, tell me in writing. You said you wanted all or nothing, but you never gave me the choice. I want you to ask me for all—that is, if you want me. You know, one of those forever kind of things.

Please let me know soon.

Love (and I mean that),

                                                    Lucy

She returned to the office with the napkin. She wanted to rewrite it on nice stationery, but knew she'd revise and revise until it wasn't as honest or bold, so she tucked the napkin in an overnight envelope with her sketches and addressed it to Chris—sealed with a kiss.

BY FRIDAY, Lucy was sure there was a secret strike at Federal Express; that was why she hadn't gotten a response. Not to mention sabotage of the phone lines. She checked both on an hourly basis.

"You ready to go to lunch yet?" Vicki asked, crossing her arms as she leaned against the front of the desk. "I'm starved."

"Let me check one more—"

"Lucy! Get a grip on yourself. Have you no pride anymore?"

"No, none at all." She dialed the number, and the Federal Express operator assured her all deliveries were on time. Again.

"I'm taking you out of town for the weekend. Maybe to one of those spa places we've been talking about going to for absolutely ever."

Lucy paced in front of the window. "I'm not sure I feel up to it."

Vicki cringed. "Geez, you'd think I asked you to join the army."

A knock sounded on the door, and Edie poked her head in. "Lucy, you have a...visitor."

The door opened, and Lucy's knees buckled as Chris walked in. He was wearing white pants and a green cotton shirt like the one she wore to bed every night. And his shark's-tooth necklace. He looked totally out of place, and completely gorgeous. Behind him, she glimpsed a few people hovering in the background, wondering who the stranger was, no doubt.

Lucy gripped the desk. "Chris," she said on a breath. "Is it really you? Or am I hallucinating?"

"I think it's me." He patted himself, smiling. "Yeah, I guess it really is." He nodded toward her. "That's probably the way I looked when you came back to Nassau."

Vicki cleared her throat, walking on enviously steady legs to Chris and extended her hand. "I'm Vicki. It's nice to meet you. Lucy's only talked about you a little...every second of the day." She shot Lucy an approving look, lifting her eyebrow. "I guess lunch is off, as well as that spa weekend, so there's no need for me to stick around. Unless, of course, you want me to..." Lucy waved her off. "Yeah, that's what I thought. Have fun, kids."

She closed the door behind her, and Lucy felt that familiar rush of warmth. She stood on wobbly legs, but he closed the distance and pulled her into his arms. She melted against him, inhaling the fresh, salt-air aroma that clung to him. Everything rushed back to her, the breezes, sunshine, moonlit nights. All that bare skin...

He cradled her face in his hands. "God, it's good to see you again."

"Better than good." She ran her fingers up by his hands and then looked at his wrist. "The bracelet's gone."

He shrugged. "It didn't do me much good after all, so I chucked it."

Her fingers tightened over his wrists. She searched his eyes for the answer to her letter, but all she saw was appreciation. "Chris, you're here..." She nodded slowly, and he did the same, waiting for her to go on. "Does that mean...I mean...you got my letter, didn't you?"

"Letter?"

Her heart dropped. "You didn't get my letter? They said you signed for it."

"My neighbor signs my name for any packages that come in while I'm gone. I flew to Hawaii right after I sent the pictures to you. You got them, didn't you?" She nodded, trying to put his presence into perspective. "The group out there that wanted me to look at the two dolphins arranged for a ticket the next day. I flew here on the way back."

She released the breath she'd been holding. "You didn't read my letter."

"I'm sorry." He cradled her closer. "You can tell me in person."

She groaned. "Why are you here?"

"Because when I got to Hawaii, I kept thinking of things to tell you, things to share with you the way we shared in Nassau. I kept hearing you asking questions, seeing your eyes filled with wonder. I knew I missed you, but I never realized how much until then. So I changed my ticket to come here. You want to know why I'm here?"

She was on the edge. "Yes."

"I came because I love you, Lucy. I can't live without you." He glanced around at the finery of her office, the view of the city beyond. "I can't give you this. I can't offer you the good life, but I can offer you my love, adventure, fulfillment, travel and a partnership of a different kind. You and me first, Lucy. Then the dolphins. But you have to know they're a part of the deal. Ah, why are you crying?"

She threw herself into his arms, hot tears flowing down her cheeks. "These were sad tears I've been holding in ever since I left Nassau. You just turned them into happy tears, and it feels so good to be happy again."

He held her close for a few minutes and then pulled back to look at her tearstained face. "Are you saying yes?" He blinked, as if he wasn't sure he'd heard her correctly.

"Are you asking me to marry you?"

"You know my policy, Miz Lucy—all or nothing."

"Then the answer is all. Yes, yes, yes!"

"But this was too easy. I thought I'd have to work harder to convince you, tell you I was wrong to think I could treat you like a dolphin and go on without you."

"You'll understand when you get my letter."

He kissed her in the way she'd been dreaming of every night, long and languorously. She tasted the salt of her tears and it reminded her of their saltwater kisses in the ocean.

"Are you sure?" he asked when he pulled back again. "I mean, this is nice. This is what you're used to. You've seen what I'm used to."

"You think this is sudden, this decision." She shook her head. "I've been thinking of nothing else since I returned. I had a long talk with my partner the morning I got the photographs. And I realized what I want is you, to be with you and work with the dolphins. I don't care if everyone thinks I'm crazy—and they will. All I care about is being happy, and being happy means being with you."

"Ah, Miz Lucy." He swiped at his eyes, and she saw they were misty. "You want to come down to Nassau with me tomorrow and see if we can find Liberty?"

"Anywhere, Chris. The good places and the bad, the paperwork and the fights with government agencies, as long as I'm with you."

His eyes sparkled like the Caribbean waters. "What say we get married while we're there? Nassau does have sentimental value, after all."

"To be sure," she said with a grin. "Bailey and Bill can be our witnesses." She pulled out copies of the artwork she'd sent him. "What do you think?"

"You did this?"

"Yep. Told you it was all I could think about."

He hugged her again. "You're incredible."

"Let's get out of here. You can show me how incredible I am. Oh my gosh, I've got to tell my parents, Tom... everyone." Her look of trepidation turned into a smile. "I don't care. I'll tell them when I get back from Nassau."

"When *we* get back from Nassau. Remember, we're a team now."

"Ooh, I love you." She kissed the tip of his nose and pulled his hand toward the door.

He surprised her by swooping her up the way he'd done that day at the beach before they'd made love the first time. Like the movie, she realized, the one she'd wanted to live. She opened the door, and he carried her through. Her arms were looped around his neck, and she snuggled up to him.

"Lucy, there's a call—" Edie stopped, phone in hand and mouth wide open.

"I'm taking the day off, Edie. No, the rest of the decade off! Forever off!" She kicked up her feet, making one of her pumps hang precariously from her toe.

Edie smiled. "So he's the reason you've been down since you came back from vacation."

"I'm not down anymore."

"I can see that." Edie returned to the phone. "Er, I'm afraid Ms. Donovan is a little...up in arms right now. Can I take a message?"

When they turned toward the lobby, they nearly ran into Tom. With a subtle signal, Chris let her slide down to her feet.

"Tom, I want you to meet Chris, the man I was telling you about. The man I'm going to marry this weekend."

The two men shook hands. Tom was openly studying Chris, who didn't seem bothered by the scrutiny.

Tom turned to her. "Does this mean—"

"Yep. We'll discuss the terms of your buying me out when we get back from Nassau this weekend. We're going to be involved in a little joint venture down there with a small hotel, and I'll be the publicity director for the Free Dolphin Society. Congratulate me, Tom. I found Lucy."

He turned to Chris. "Take good care of her."

Chris tightened his arm around her. "Oh, I plan to."

"Well, Tom, if you don't mind, I've got a little fantasy to live out." Chris swooped her back up into his arms. "Ciao."

Epilogue

One year later...

"WELL, WHAT DO YOU THINK?" Lucy handed Chris the letter she'd drafted to the government of Antigua. They had recently banned Matt Adamson's entrance into the country to educate the public about a new dolphin swim program. Matt was one of their new associates, along with a secretary. They now operated out of a storefront space in a nearby shopping plaza.

Chris took the letter out onto the small deck that overlooked the beach. She'd been amused to see that his "small" place in the Keys was a stilt house right on the Atlantic Ocean. Oh, it was small, at least in comparison to the apartment she'd sold in Minneapolis. But it was plenty big enough for the two of them. Though she had added her woman's touch to his home, he wouldn't let her put much of her money into either the house or the organization. She suspected that he was afraid she'd come to her senses and head back to her other world. When he thought she was asleep, he voiced those fears: *I don't know what I'd do without you, Lucy.* She had some news that would forever squash his doubts.

She joined her husband on the deck and slid her arms around his waist.

"Great job," he said, kissing the top of her head.

"Then I think it deserves more of a kiss than that."

He obliged, capturing her mouth and giving her an up-one-side-down-the-other kind of kiss. His tongue teased, darting around her teeth and tickling the roof of her mouth. He finished with a gentle nibble on her lower lip. He had kept his promise: never once had he put the dolphins before her. They were a team, and she had given her soul to the dolphins as surely as he had. He, of course, had the biggest place in her heart.

A seagull squawked as it swooped past their deck. Even though the sun was setting on the other coast, the sky to the east was splashed in hues of pink and blue. Though she'd decided to tell him on their trip to Nassau the following week to check on Liberty and celebrate their first anniversary, this was a perfect moment. Besides, she couldn't wait another minute.

"I won't be able to go with you and Matt to Curacao this fall." They were scheduled to talk with the government about a possible captive dolphin swim program. She held her breath at the question in his eyes. "I'm pregnant."

They hadn't talked about children yet. They'd been too busy discovering each other, making love and, as it turned out, making a baby.

His fingers tightened on her waist as shock overtook his features. "P-p-pregnant?"

She nodded, afraid to show him just how excited she was about it. "The pill's not one hundred percent accurate. I'll still help out as much as I can, and I know you've got to keep things going—"

He picked her up and swung her around. "You're going to have a baby. *We're* going to have a baby!" He kissed her again, and then he set her down and touched her belly. "When did you find out? When is the baby due? How? Why?"

She laughed as her eyes welled up. He wasn't mad or disappointed. In fact, his eyes were tearing up, too. "Three days ago, in about eight months, the usual way and because we're lucky."

He squeezed her in a bear hug. "*I'm* lucky."

"You're not upset? I mean, it will change our lives. The dolphins won't come second. They'll be third. The baby will be first."

"Our family comes first, Lucy. That's the way it is, whether that family is just us or three or even four of us. I've been thinking about this—"

She took a step back. "You have?"

"You didn't think I expected you to give up everything, did you? When I think what you gave up to be with me..." He shook his head. "You amaze me. When I fell in love with you...when I decided I couldn't live without you...I knew I couldn't ask you to give up motherhood, too. I'd planned to talk to you about it down in the Bahamas. Matt and I have been discussing it and—"

"You've been talking about having a baby *with Matt?*"

He laughed, and then she laughed when she realized what she'd said. "Didn't you think you should talk to me first?"

He gathered her in his arms again, and as indignant as she wanted to be, she just couldn't manage it. He said, "I wanted to set things up. You and I will handle the paperwork end of the organization, and Matt will handle all of the travel part. Remember when we talked about buying a boat? I thought we'd do that, and I'll take people out to swim with dolphins in their natural habitat. That way I'm educating people *and* making money. And we're home. We'll make this a home." He pulled her tight against him. "We're going to be a real family."

"We already are a family." She closed her eyes and

sank into his warmth. She knew what he was giving up, too. But they would gain so much more in return, just as she had gained so much when she'd given up her life in Minneapolis.

Chris leaned back. "We'll get a dog. And a parrot. We'll close in the bottom floor and make it a big playroom."

She'd never heard him talk so much! She ruffled his hair. "Are you sure you want this? You sound so hesitant."

She thought he'd laugh, but he framed her face with his hands and looked so very serious. "For a long time, I didn't think I wanted a wife or a family. I thought that I only wanted to live for the dolphins. You changed all that. You changed me. When you gave up that successful life you had up north to be with me, you changed my mind about a lot of things. I want this, and I want you...forever."

"Well, good, because you're stuck with me forever."

He pulled her close, his mouth hovering over hers. "Now, Miz Lucy, that is something I can live with." And then he kissed her crazy.

* * * * *

Don't miss Tina Wainscott's
latest and wackiest romantic comedy,
DRIVEN TO DISTRACTION
published by Harlequin Duets
August 2002.

This is the family reunion you've been waiting for!

TRUEBLOOD
Christmas

JASMINE CRESSWELL
TARA TAYLOR QUINN
& KATE HOFFMANN

deliver three brand new Trueblood, Texas stories.

After many years, Major Brad Henderson is released from prison, exonerated after almost thirty years for a crime he didn't commit. His mission: to be reunited with his three daughters. How to find them? Contact Dylan Garrett of the Finders Keepers Detective Agency!

Look for it in November 2002.

HARLEQUIN®
Makes any time special®

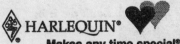

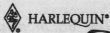

HARLEQUIN®
Duets™

Ready to take on the world—and some unsuspecting men—these red-hot royals are looking for love and fun in *all* the right places!

Don't miss four new stories by two of Duets hottest authors!

RED-HOT ROYALS

Once Upon a Tiara
Henry Ever After

by Carrie Alexander
September 2002

A Royal Mess
Her Knight
To Remember

by Jill Shalvis
October 2002

Available at your favorite retail outlet.

HARLEQUIN®
Makes any time special ®

Visit us at www.eHarlequin.com

HDRHR

Princes...Princesses...
London Castles...New York Mansions...
To live the life of a royal!

In 2002, Harlequin Books lets you escape to a world of royalty with these royally themed titles:

Temptation:
January 2002—*A Prince of a Guy* (#861)
February 2002—*A Noble Pursuit* (#865)

American Romance:
The Carradignes: American Royalty (Editorially linked series)
March 2002—*The Improperly Pregnant Princess* (#913)
April 2002—*The Unlawfully Wedded Princess* (#917)
May 2002—*The Simply Scandalous Princess* (#921)
November 2002—*The Inconveniently Engaged Prince* (#945)

Intrigue:
The Carradignes: A Royal Mystery (Editorially linked series)
June 2002—*The Duke's Covert Mission* (#666)

Chicago Confidential
September 2002—*Prince Under Cover* (#678)

The Crown Affair
October 2002—*Royal Target* (#682)
November 2002—*Royal Ransom* (#686)
December 2002—*Royal Pursuit* (#690)

Harlequin Romance:
June 2002—*His Majesty's Marriage* (#3703)
July 2002—*The Prince's Proposal* (#3709)

Harlequin Presents:
August 2002—*Society Weddings* (#2268)
September 2002—*The Prince's Pleasure* (#2274)

Duets:
September 2002—*Once Upon a Tiara/Henry Ever After* (#83)
October 2002—*Natalia's Story/Andrea's Story* (#85)

**Celebrate a year of royalty with
Harlequin Books!**

Available at your favorite retail outlet.

♦ **HARLEQUIN**®
Makes any time special ®

Visit us at www.eHarlequin.com

HSROY02